Viscera

Viscera

AN ANTHOLOGY OF BIZARRE EROTICA

Edited by Cara Bruce

Viscera

First Printing 2000
ISBN 0-9673638-0-2

Cover Art by Trevor Brown
Cover Design by Bonnie Barrett
Book Design by David Van Ness

A version of "Petty Intrusion" first appeared in *Noirotica 2: Pulp Friction* (Masquerade, 1997)
"Knife" first appeared in *Leatherwoman* (Masquerade, 1993)

Manufactured in Canada

Published by Venus or Vixen Press
PO Box 591257
San Francisco, CA 94159-1257
http://www.venusorvixen.com

ACKNOWLEDGEMENTS

I would like to thank the following people for their guidance and support: Paul Cafaro, Paula Guran, Thomas S. Roche, Marcy Sheiner, Missy Axelrod, Suzi Pastorelli, and Michaela Conway. I would like to particularly acknowledge Dani Bauter for all of her help and friendship. Most of all I would like to thank my family for everything you've ever done. And I mean that as a compliment.

CONTENTS

INTRODUCTION

"You know about the detachable heads, don't you?"

—Baron Munchausen

In this part of the film Baron Munchausen is talking about the moon king, who constantly tries to separate his head from his body; disgusted by his own base desires and wanting to follow "otherworldly pursuits." The age-old argument of body versus intellect rears its ugly head. But in real life one helps the other: our minds eroticize so our bodies can feel. Sometimes when our minds tell us things are bad it makes them more desirable, granting us the taboo.

Many of the stories in *Viscera* focus on taboo, erotica and death: the taboos of necrophilia, of blasphemous religious symbols and murder, all presented with their polar opposite—the lifegiving force of sex. Pleasure mixed with pain, as well as shame, grief and fear.

When I came up with the idea for *Viscera* I was feeling numb—attempting to shut out pain. I daydreamed about throwing myself through windows and being cut with glass just to feel something. I also fucked like a banshee. I had sex more frequently, rougher and harder than I ever had in my life. All in the hopes of feeling something. I figured if neither the fear of death nor the pleasure in sex could make me feel again I didn't know what could.

To be safe I decided to combine the two.

I asked for sick stories. I asked for murder, disgust and, of course, sex. I wanted pain, suffering, blood, guts, or just plain weirdness. Instead most of the stories I got made me laugh. They were so ridiculous I couldn't help it: from a modern day Salome to a decapitation party; a frat boy's date gone horribly wrong to a lonely night at the morgue. I thought I had needed to feel more pain to heal, or to feel the pain I thought I deserved. I didn't. I needed to laugh.

Nevertheless, a good portion of *Viscera* is eerily beautiful or downright creepy. These stories are the ones that will probably turn you on when you pull up the covers and snuggle into bed with this book. So go ahead—if nothing else, I hope I make you feel something.

Cara Bruce
San Francisco, 1999

PURE LOVE

Simon Sheppard

I loved him so much it made my pussy ache.

I'd go down to the basement, where Daddy kept him tied up. I'd look at his naked, bound-up body, coils of rope pressing into dead-white flesh, and love him so much, just fucking love him so much. He made me feel the hollowness inside me, he was the child I'd gotten rid of, he was my God, my very own naked, tied-up God.

And did he care? Did he accept my love?

Not on your fucking life. He'd lecture me, call me a Sodomite, like in the Bible. Told me I was bad, that women always were bad, ever since Goddamn Eve in the Garden of Goddamn Eden. The fucking uptight cocksucker.

Weird thing, though. The more he insulted me, the hotter I got. The more I loved him. Go figure.

I'd play with him, take some rope and tie it around the base of his dick and balls, watch his big, cut dick get good and hard. And then I'd try to kiss him. Only try. 'Cause sure, our lips met, but I never got any tongue. Fucking uptight bastard. BOY, did I love him!

I loved him so much that when I lay in bed at night, all I could do was think of him down in the basement. Didn't he get it? How much I adored him, how much I could mean to him? I'd think and think and think about him, till finally I'd have to rub my cunt just so I could relax and get some sleep.

I mean I really, really loved him. I absolutely knew he was meant for me, God meant for us to be together. Always. Y'know? Plus, he really, really looked hunky in all that rope. I'd never been into the bondage thing till Daddy tied him up. But when I'd go down to feed him or something and I saw him all tied-up against the cinder block wall, it got me real wet. After I'd fed him, I'd take off my jeans and get down on all fours, show him my pussy, tell him I'd be his little puppy-dog, his very own hot bitch, forever and ever and ever.

You think he cared? Shit no. He'd go on and on about how bad I was and he'd rag on my mom and dad. I guess I just didn't make myself clear or something. See, I knew he was meant to be the love of my life. He was sent to me so he and I could be together always, only he didn't get it.

And one way or another, I meant to have him. The lousy bastard. The lousy, hunky bastard.

So one night when we're all together, watching TV, I ask my daddy if I could have a favor.

"Can I have a favor, Daddy?"

"What's that, hon?"

"I'll tell you later."

"Then how can I know if I'll do you the favor?"

"How about if I dance for you, Daddy? Will you do me the favor then?"

Mom shoots me a look. But I can tell I got the Old Man hooked.

"How about if I dance really, really good for you? Will you do it then?"

"Um...um...yeah, sure."

"Anything?"

"Not the car, you can't have the car tonight."

"Okay, not the car. But you'll do anything else I ask you to?"

"Sure."

"Promise?"

"Promise."

"Cross your heart and hope to die?"

Mom shoots me another look, even nastier this time, but goes right back to watching the junk on TV.

"...and hope to die."

So I run upstairs and get some scarves and stuff out of my closet, and wrap them around me like they're some kind of hootchie-cootchie costume or something. And when I get back downstairs, Mom's gone to the kitchen, but Dad's sitting there in the Barcalounger looking towards the stairs and his hands are in his lap.

I want to turn off the TV, which has one of those really junky comedy shows on, but Daddy says, "No, Mommy'll be right back," so I start to dance for him, really sexy. Or as sexy as I *can* be with all those people in the TV audience laughing their stupid heads off about some really fucking stupid joke or other. I twirl around and get real close to him and every so often pull off one of the scarves and get even closer and rub up against him and then twirl away again. And all the while the TV is going hahahahaha and then there's a commercial and I pull off my T-shirt and since I'm not wearing a bra, Daddy can see my tits, so I squeeze them together and kinda milk them and then play with the nipples and just then Mom comes back in with a bag of low-fat microwave popcorn, just when I'm playing with my nipples. She sits back down and watches TV like nothing else is happening and then TV finishes selling cunt deodorant or something and the hahaha starts again just when I'm unbuttoning my jeans. I pull 'em off and I'm down to my panties and my dad can't take his fucking eyes off me and I notice, actually I noticed a long time ago, that his hands are twisting around in his lap and kind of playing with his thing real good. And you may think the whole thing is kind of gross, but remember I'm not really dancing for my dad, I'm dancing for the guy downstairs, and I don't see my father sitting there, see, I see my one true love sitting there, only he's naked and tied to the chair, tied down real good like one of those big-boob bimbos in my father's magazines. I see him sitting there with his legs tied so his thighs are wide apart and his big stiff thing is pointing at me and his hands are tied back so he's helpless and I can do anything I want to him, which is basically to love him, I can assure you. To love him.

Only remember, it's not really him sitting there, it's my dad, and by the time I've got one of the scarves in my hands, running it between my legs and rubbing my pussy with it through the panties, by then Dad's got his thing out, and he's playing with it, and it's not as nice as my lover's, let me tell you. Not nearly. And Mom is still pretending to watch TV, but she's looking at us out of the corner of her eye, checking out what's happening. And I twirl away one last time, pull my panties off, and dance up to my dad and sit down on him, straddling his leg and rubbing myself against him, riding his leg like you'd ride a pony. And my hand's right on his thing, which feels pretty hot and hard.

"So you'll do me a favor, Daddy?" My hand starts stroking up and down on his thing.

"Yeah, yeah. Whaddya want?" he gasps. His voice sounds real funny.

"I want the guy's head," I say.

"You want him to give you *head*?" Dad can be kind of dense sometimes.

"No, Daddy, I want you to go down and cut off his head and bring it back upstairs to me."

Mom is looking kind of funny, but she's afraid to say anything. As usual.

I take my hand away and Daddy says, "Do me more," but I say, "No, first you go down and cut the guy's head off and then we'll see."

So he puts his thing back and goes out the front door and I hear the garage door open and he comes back carrying his axe and he heads down to the basement.

Mom reaches for the remote and turns the sound up real loud, I guess so she can't hear anything else, and now the hahaha is over and it's a cop show and the gunshots sound really loud, like they were in our own living room or something.

And when Dad comes back upstairs he's carrying a big plastic dish like you'd put under a potted plant. Only there's not a plant on the dish, there's the head. Dad hadn't actually made too bad a job of it, my lover's neck isn't too messy, not too chewed-up or anything, and his skin looks real, real white against the blood sloshing around in the bottom of the green plastic dish.

"Okay, little girl, now you finish what you started with me, okay?"

"Later, Daddy."

"NOW, you little bitch."

"Now, *dear*..." says my mom to my dad.

I just smile and say, "Which would you rather, Daddy, that I finish you later, or that I tell the police what you just did?"

And Dad shuts up real quick.

So I carry the head up to my bedroom and lock the door and put the dish down on my bed and start talking to him like he can still hear me.

"You wouldn't let me kiss you but now I'm gonna kiss you and there's not a fucking thing you can do about it and now you're going to know that I really, really love you and that I'm the love of your life." Stuff like that.

I grab his head and bend down and kiss his mouth, which is still sorta warm. It tastes kinda bitter, but I don't think it's the blood, because I know what blood tastes like, since sometimes I get my own pussy blood on my fingers and lick them clean. That tastes salty and this tastes kind of bitter. So I decide it's the taste of love, the bitter taste of love. I think I heard that somewhere. Maybe it's a song.

Only I can't get my tongue in his mouth till I pry open his jaws, which isn't really that hard to do. And then I kiss him way deep and hard and I know for sure that I'll always really, really love him.

I'd pulled my panties back on while Dad was down in the basement, and now when I start rubbing myself against my love's head the blood starts soaking my panties like I was on the biggest period of all time. But I don't mind.

Then I get an idea, so I pull off my panties again and throw them in the wastebasket so the blood won't get on anything, even though the bedspread is already getting kind of messy. And then I reach into his mouth and pull his tongue out as best I can, and since it's slippery and kind of stiff, I can't do it too good. But I've got his head lying there with the tip of his tongue stuck out, and I straddle his head like I straddled my dad's leg, only it's like my lover is eating me out. I hold his head and move it around until his tongue is in just the right spot, and then pretty quick I'm coming and coming and coming. And I scream out, "I LOVE YOU. I LOVE YOU SO MUCH."

And a little later I go down to the basement and Daddy

hasn't cleaned up at all yet. It's still really messy. The axe is lying there, and so is my love, without his head of course, but lying there tied up and naked. So I go over and try to stick my hand down into where his head had been, like I'm reaching down into him to grab his heart, like it's my valentine or something. I can't do it, of course, so I take the axe, but it's really hard to chop into a guy's chest, so pretty soon I give up.

But I know that, in a funny way, his heart will *always* be mine, 'cause I'll always love him.

'Cause I love him so much it makes my fucking pussy ache.

BEDROOM VIROLOGY

Thomas S. Roche

As she undresses in front of the mirror, she can see the outline of her pale flesh flickering. She takes off her suit coat, her skirt, kicks off her shoes. She unbuttons her blouse and stands in the blue-white light as it washes in waves, on-off-on—like lightning—over her half-clothed body.

"…stolen from a San Francisco hotel room earlier today. Police officials say this is not a general health threat for the people of San Francisco, but could be a threat…"

She shrugs off the blouse, runs her hands down her body. Neatly hooks her panties and slides them down. Takes the bra off last; she's always liked the way her breasts look in underwire. Slowly, she unhooks it, eases it over her tits. Her nipples are erect.

"…for whoever discovers the vial. The vial contains cultures…"

She shrugs off the bra. She takes a step back from the

mirror, watches herself while she plays with her tits a little, while she runs her hand down the inside of her slightly-spread thighs. She slips a finger inside. She is dripping.

"...consists of a glass vial approximately two and one half inches across and eight inches wide. The vial contains a white gelatinous substance which is the medium for the virus culture..."

Still standing, she reaches out to where she's laid the thick glass tube on the counter beside the sink. God, it's fucking huge. Can she even take it? She purses her lips, licks two fingers with her swollen, hungry tongue and sticks them neatly inside her pussy. She moans softly as she feels her flesh closing around her fingers. Tight. Unyielding. But desirous.

"...vial *is* considered fragile, and if dropped could shatter, releasing the virus into the air..."

She inverts the thick glass vial, with one hand holding the plastic airtight lid, with the other—using just two fingers—guiding the head of the thing to the uppermost juncture of her lips. She starts teasing her clit, moaning softly and then louder as she draws the head around her erect member in little circles. It's ridiculous to call it a head—it's a smooth cylinder, its bottom rounded just so... perfect for fitting into tight spaces...

Why did she take it? It's not like she needs the money, not really. But she *had* to—that doctor was stupid enough not to check her hotel door as she left. You should *always* check hotel doors. And she'd left the door just a slight bit ajar... oh, she couldn't have just *left* it there, half-open, or maybe not half-open, but a little bit open at least... that would have been such a waste, to walk by without *exploring* a little. And then, once she was in the doctor's room, among her things, among her dirty underwear on the bed and her disarrayed luggage... feeling the woman's aura shot through the room, smelling her expensive perfume, once she'd seen the monogrammed leather bag. Well, how the fuck was she to know the doctor was a researcher? She'd just wanted to look through the bag, just to *know* she'd stolen it. But then, when she saw the vial, saw its simply too-perfect dimensions...

But of course, the moment she had known she was going to do it was the moment she heard the first news broadcast.

She'd been fighting this war with herself since childhood. Kleptomania, the doctors called it. But she knew better. It wasn't just kleptomania. It was an addiction to risk. An addiction to danger.

She has her own name for it: Kleptophilia. What better way to consummate her union with danger, with theft? The best criminals do it for love, not money.

She watches herself in the flickering light, listens to her panting moans mingling with the news broadcast. It feels like the thing's got a mind of its own—like the cultures inside are directing her actions, like the collective mind of the deadliest virus on the planet is fucking her—just as eager to screw her as she is to be screwed. But no, she tells herself that's impossible. She has to guide the tip of the vial to her pussy.

She lets the vial nuzzle its way into the entrance to her cunt. Rocks back on her heels, takes a deep breath, lets it out as she pushes the vial home. Feels the tightness of her cunt resisting. Moans—in mingled pain, pleasure, and terror—as she feels the thing entering her, penetrating her. For a second she thinks she's going to pull it out, it's going to hurt her—but no, she gets it in. God, her pussy feels tight. Christ, that thing feels big in there. If she clamped her pussy-muscles down now, she'd pop the thing like a balloon. Shatter it, shred her flesh, inject herself with death. She'd crash and bleed before she finished coming.

But no—she's going to come. She keeps fucking herself with the vial. It takes a dozen thrusts, hard thrusts into her while she works her clit, a dozen hard thrusts—then two dozen, then another dozen in rapid succession as she throws back her head and screams. Just as she reaches her climax she realizes her muscles are going to implode with tension—and the fear seizes her just at the moment her orgasm explodes through her. She totters on her feet as she hears the shattering glass—then as her head spins with asphyxia, her knees give way and she falls, hard on her ass, thrusting her hips up at the very last instant—

"...that's right, I'll say it again! We're *smashing* low prices!"

The sound of breaking glass.

She can't have been out for more than a minute. She shudders in fear and relief as she feels her ass against the hard, cold linoleum floor of the cheap motel bathroom. So cheap there's not even a door—so she can see the plaid-jacketed used-car salesman throwing a sledgehammer through the window.

Delicately, she feels the entrance to her pussy, terror shivering inside her. But the only wetness she feels is her juice, leaking out of her as she eases the thick vial out of her cunt.

"As a follow-up to our previous story: Tonight, police and public health officials are asking what a top-level researcher was doing travelling with a vial full of deadly virus cultures...."

She knows what the good Doctor was doing with it. Engaging in a little virophilia. Nothing like a little bedroom virology to get the blood moving.

Softly, she smiles. Stands up, walks to the bed. Tucks the vial, its outside slick with her secretions, under the pillow. Sits on the side of the bed, naked, and lights a cigarette. Smokes it, feeling the afterspasms of her orgasm.

"Repeat our earlier bulletin: A vial of potentially deadly virus cultures has been stolen from a San Francisco hotel room."

She hits the remote control; the TV flickers and dies.

Methodically, she slides her stockings up her legs, hooks her garter belt and attaches them. Puts on her bra, climbs into her skirt and blouse. Packs her things in her single shoulder bag, slings it over her shoulder; tucks her clutch purse under her arm. Turns off the light. Exits the hotel room, leaving the vial under the pillow. Closes the door behind her.

She finds a house phone and dials 9-1-1.

Later, walking briskly down the corridor to the terminal, forty minutes before her flight, she pauses in mid-step, her heart beating faster all of a sudden, her breath catching in her throat. She finds a chair and her purse on the little ledge beside it. She rifles through her purse, takes out her wallet.

She digs until she finds the hotel check-in receipt.

Takes out the identification and credit card.

Checks the numbers carefully, just to make sure they aren't hers. She smiles, takes a deep breath, mops her brow with a discarded towel she finds on the counter.

She puts her wallet away, slings her shoulder bag, puts her clutch purse under her arm again. Walks to the gate smiling and humming to herself, a spring in her step.

THE DECAPITATION PARTY

Paul Bradshaw

Cedric just wasn't the same after being decapitated. He sat in the armchair, headless and immobile, with warm blood bubbling from the gaping point of separation. I had never known him to be so silent, and I recall thinking to myself: *I ought to have beheaded my husband a long time ago.*

Samantha was the first to arrive. I wasn't really surprised, for I always regarded her as the most inquisitive of my close friends. Cedric remained in the chair, as I didn't have the heart to remove his lifeless form, and what's more I didn't possess the strength to do so.

"Where is he then?" Samantha inquired with a sinister enthusiasm, rushing past me through the hallway and heading directly for the lounge.

I had placed the head on the coffee table beside the armchair, after I had composed myself of course. Immediately after I had committed the foul deed I found that my body was shaking violently. A claret pool spread across the formica, and I conjectured that an abnormal amount of cleaning would eventually be required. I watched Samantha intently; curious as to how she would react upon discovering Cedric in his headless state.

"Oh, my God!" she screamed, and I was almost forced to laugh facetiously, for her facial expression was both incredulous and fantastic.

"You didn't believe me, did you?" I said.

She shook her head, apparently horror-stricken and unable to speak, standing stark still mere feet from the deceased body slumped in the chair. His blood trickled over his neck and onto his shirt, dark red and as thick as treacle.

"What made you do it, Lucy?" she asked with a trembling voice, obviously having regained her speaking abilities.

I recreated the events of the three hours previously in my mind, before beginning to relate the freak occurrence to my friend. It began like this: Cedric disturbingly preferred the television to my company. Indeed, he was in the act of watching some inane trash when the argument started. We seemed to quarrel more and more as the weeks passed, but I never expected our verbal combat to reach such a delirious conclusion.

"But surely that's not reason to slick off his head," debated Samantha.

"Perhaps not, but let me finish my story."

Most times our contentious exchange of views resorted to sex. I don't mean we ended up wrapped in each other's arms and overcome with a morbid passion, as I regard that both foolhardy and unexciting. No, my meaning is that we began to argue on that subject, and that was when things got distressingly chaotic. Cedric revealed some frightful and sickening home truths concerning our shared intimacies, and I found myself buried beneath an avalanche of emotion.

"So what happened?" asked Samantha.

I then knew she was back to her usual prying self, as she was practically begging with her eyes for me to relinquish the gory details. However, before I was able to describe the bloodshed that took place in the lounge I heard the doorbell sound a second time. This caused us both to literally jump in fright, and I sort of half-expected Cedric to do the same, but then I realized how silly that particular notion was.

It was my other friend Rachel, and I beckoned her inside, taking the bottle of wine she presented to me. I was shocked to receive such an offering, but then it dawned on me that the gathering I had arranged following the gruesome slaying—the get-together procured by way of a series of surreptitious telephone calls—could indeed be classed as an unholy celebration of my newly-discovered freedom.

"Jesus!" cried Rachel upon viewing Cedric's corpse, and she collapsed on to the settee. "I think I need a drink."

I obliged; as a matter of fact I hadn't realized until then that I too required a shot of some alcohol-based beverage.

"Put some music on," Samantha urged me.

I found the proceedings most macabre at that point, as I selected Lionel Richie from my extensive compact disc collection. The wine, the music, the brandy that Rachel and I began to share; it was turning into a party, an unnatural celebration of my husband's savage death.

I continued the devilish tale I was recounting to Samantha just prior to Rachel's arrival. It was one of those long-handled axes that Cedric kept in the garage for some unknown reason I could never understand, as he never seemed to use the implement. The hefty tool was quite sharp, but even then it took some minutes before the head was severed completely. Although my heart was pounding inside my chest I committed the act with great ease and abandon with little thought of the agonizing consequences, both for myself and for Cedric. It was only after I placed his dripping head upon the table that I came to my senses, and dashed to the bathroom to vomit horrendously.

"So what happens now?" asked Samantha.

"God knows. I just feel so confused."

Rachel was silently demolishing the brandy, eyeing Cedric's cold features as she drank her way to oblivion. She was certainly the quiet type, and I didn't expect any hysterics from her. In fact I reckoned the both of them were taking the whole thing rather calmly. I wondered how my third friend would react to facing the decapitated Cedric.

"I'm sorry I couldn't get here sooner," explained Melinda as she crossed the threshold with a bottle of Pinot Noir in her hand, "Glenn insisted on giving me a good rogering before I left. You know what he's like!"

Melinda was bubbly and energetic, and completely gorgeous. I'd lost count of how many men she'd been involved with, but every one of them was a nefarious character in some way or another. She always dressed in as little clothing as she could get away with, and underwear was entirely out of the question as far as she was concerned.

"Let's see then, is it true?" she remarked as she made her way along the hallway. "Oh, Lucy. I don't believe it!"

It was all rather weird. Lionel Richie was singing, Samantha was observing Cedric with a terrible awe, Rachel was guzzling the spirit, and Melinda was standing in front of my unfortunate partner. My trio of friends, all sharing my horrible grief. At that moment I felt most relieved to have such faithful companions.

"You well and truly did it then, didn't you Lucy?" said Melinda. "Come on, get that booze out. Let's have a party!"

She was insatiable, dressed in her little white dress, her high heels, and nothing much else. From that moment on we began to really let our hair down. I put on more raucous music, Rachel organized the spirits and the wine, and Samantha remained with Cedric, reluctant to leave him for some unspeakable reason, bearing a strange fascination for his bleeding head and the stump of his neck.

"It must have taken a lot of guts to do such a thing," said Samantha, her eyes still fixed on Cedric's decapitated head.

"That's right," said Melinda, "I wouldn't mind doing the same to Glenn, although it wouldn't affect his brain that much."

As I admired the subtlety of her fiendish joke I found myself recalling yet again the gross misdeed I had performed earlier; it was difficult to erase such a wrongdoing from my mind. I pictured an image of myself swinging the bloodied axe time after time, connecting with Cedric's opened neck, the awful gurgling sounds that emanated from the back of his throat. Then Samantha interrupted my thoughts.

"Oh, my God!" she cried, "His eyes moved!"

We all turned abruptly to face Cedric's head. At first I thought it was the drink causing her eyes to play tricks on her, but the events that followed proved my supposition to be incorrect.

"That's impossible," said Melinda. "There's no way his eyes could move."

"You're imagining things," I pointed out to her.

"Look!" Rachel suddenly screamed, pointing to my deceased husband's groin area.

Our attentions were then turned in that direction, and I was horrified to observe the unique protuberance at the front of his trousers.

"Christ, he's got a hard-on!" said Melinda.

"He can't have," I protested, "I've never heard of that happening before, have you? It's so weird."

Trust Melinda to be the one to investigate, as she knelt before Cedric and began to unzip him. I cringed at her outlandish behavior, blaming the demon drink for her apparent waywardness. Then I gasped, for there before the four of us was Cedric's abnormal blue veiner.

"I've heard of rigor mortis but this is ridiculous," joked Melinda, as she held the hardness in her hand. Then I spotted a certain mischief in her eyes. "How about if I give him one last hand job?"

Samantha shrieked with morbid laughter, "I bet you wouldn't."

Melinda was true to her word as she started to masturbate Cedric's posthumous erection, her hand gripping him and moving up and down rapidly. I myself was thunderstruck at such a forbidding act, and I viewed the freakish goings-on with disbelief.

"I dare you to suck it," said Samantha.

Melinda was such a capricious person I wasn't sure whether she would adhere to the suggestion, but she must have surely been in a party mood that night because she indeed became tempted to absorb the dead penis within her hungry mouth. However, that was not the end of the night's proceedings, not by a long shot, for further chilling incidents awaited the four of us, incidents that would prove to change the course of our lives in a hellish manner.

I myself was naturally astounded when I witnessed Cedric's arms miraculously return to life, his hands clasping Melinda's head to shove her face further into his groin. Needless to say I was unable to comprehend the horror of the situation at that point in time. The three of us appeared to cry out in unison, obviously shocked at such a fascinating occurrence. What happened next only intensified the weirdness of the situation.

"Look at his face," yelled Rachel, who was still brandishing the bottle of brandy, "his eyes are moving and so is his mouth."

She was correct; his face had also magically assumed a living countenance, the twitching of the eyebrows, and the protrusion of his tongue upon his lips unmistakable. I began to consider what other sinister happenings would take place during the remainder of the evening.

As for Melinda, she started to assume the identity of some wicked vixen, for I was astonished when she ceased her oral pleasures and clambered upon Cedric's lap, hoisting her short dress to reveal no briefs, and incredibly lowering herself onto his erection to take part in a sickening act of necrophilic intercourse. Strangely I found her actions to be most erotic, as I watched with a confused interest.

With loud rock music now playing and Rachel emptying the brandy bottle with a thirsty relish, Samantha suddenly decided to join in the satanic sexual gratification. She sprang from her sitting position in the opposite armchair and snatched Cedric's head from the coffee table, then in one swift movement removed her briefs and began to use the decapitated object as some form of grotesque dildo, grinding his face between her splayed thighs. I shall never forget the inhuman expression she displayed, and I truly thought that I was trapped inside a weird nightmare. At first I refused to believe that he was actually delivering cunnilingual delights to Samantha, but when she adjusted her position slightly I spotted Cedric's tongue endeavoring to reach out for her gleaming vulva, and I shuddered at the macabre sight.

At the same time Melinda was still riding him, with his hands holding her at each side, steadying her position upon her lap. Yes, his arms were alive, and so was his head. I was naturally spellbound, imagining I had been secretly transported to some monstrous hell. My friends didn't appear to realize the haunting implications of what was happening in that room, as if a strange voodoo spell had been cast upon the three of them.

Soon it was Rachel's turn to be overcome by the carnal magic which seemed to be present that night. Melinda climbed off Cedric's knees, apparently suffering from a form of cramp, but before she was able to resume her enjoyment Rachel left the settee to take over, grabbing the still-hard cock and beginning to suck and slurp with a savage abandon, taking the whole six inches into her mouth.

Before long he ejaculated, but still Rachel kept his erection between her lips, not allowing him to withdraw until she was satisfied completely. Samantha too seemed to have finished receiving pleasure from the head, returning it to the table and pulling her briefs back on. All manner of eroticism came to a close, and a peaceful air pervaded; even the compact disc had reached its conclusion. There was no more movement from Cedric, not ever in fact, his arms resting by his sides once more, his face as cold and unnerving as before, and his dick enclosed within his trousers, limp and still. The terrifying delirium my friends had experienced had ceased, and I for one was vastly relieved.

I suppose I could have been tempted to join in the sexual reverie, to welcome a series of immensely enjoyable orgasms the like of which I had not experienced before, but such things only seem to occur in storybooks, or so I believed at the time. Little did I realize that in the near future I would partake in similar examples of astounding behavior; for yes, I was destined to attend three additional decapitation parties during the weeks that followed.

THE BANG GANG

M. Christian

It was just a bathroom—Deux couldn't tell what all the fuss was about.

It wasn't even a spectacular bathroom, as women's restrooms went. God knows she'd seen worse and better. But the way the dykes, femmes, grrls, doms, subs, daddies, little girls, and passers queued, elbowed, crammed, squeezed and fuckin' even fought to get in, you'd think the Under Club's can was gold-plated or something.

Deux couldn't care less. She just had to fucking pee.

Luckily she'd managed to tag along behind a motherfuckin' huge black butch in leather pants, leather vest, and a white T. This monstrous specimen of outrageously proportioned, masculine-tinted femininity parted the sea of dykes and femmes like Moses dipping his little pinkies in the Red Sea.

No marble, no brass, no plush carpeting on the dainty little seats. No complimentary little pastel soaps in the shape of sea shells. The Under Club's can was one huge room with a ragged seam down and around the middle—showing where the wall had been torn out between the LADIES and the original MENS. The urinals left behind were festively decorated with piles of gloves, dams and condoms—save one that was left intact and even polished. For, Deux guessed, the really, truly hardcore butches to piss in.

The place was full, but not packed. Deux took it in with a quick scope, stepping from behind Big Black Butch (who was doing the same from her vantage point a head taller than the rather diminutive Deux) the femmes were pressing and clucking in a clutch around the few free sinks, putting their faces back on and spraying their smooth-shaven pits with something sweet-smelling. The butches, meanwhile, preened their pompadours and mohawks in the steel mirrors, each one claiming a lot more personal, macho, space—spilling so far into the room that Deux could smell the Brylcream.

A few punks sat in a loose circle in the no man's land between the two old rooms, passing a brass pipe around, bobbing their blue, green, red and orange hairstyles and laughing at jokes that only they, and the pot, could understand.

Bending down, Deux scanned the bottom of the nearest row of stalls. Heels. Doc Martens. Jungle boots. Pumps. Tennis shoes. Ballet slippers.

The other side: another pair of Docs. Another pair of heels. Sandals. Bare feet. Then nothing—a free stall.

As she did a quick little trot (can't be macho running for

the bathroom) towards the stall a sudden heavy thumping seemed to follow her. Being that this was, after all, San Francisco, the first thought that raced through her head was *earthquake*. But it seemed a bit too regular, too thump-thump-thump for one of Mother Nature's temper tantrums. Then Deux looked behind her and got her answer: the Big Black Butch was right behind her, racing her for the empty stall—her boots thump-thump-thumping the tiled floor.

Just as she realized that she was a deer caught in the headlights between the sixteen-wheeler truck, that was the monster butch, and relief, which was the toilet, a hand dropped onto her shoulder. Slowly, calmly, she stopped and looked over at it. Yep, big, black and strong.

Deux considered herself a wolverine. Small, sure, but mean as all motherfuckin' hell. She might have only been 5'3" and looked too much like an elf (with her pointed ears, tiny nose, and pursed lips) but her spiritual daddy was Clint "Dirty Harry" Eastwood.

Deux was half-ready to grab the dyke in an improv karate grip when the dyke bent down from her six-something-double-digit height and said, softly, quietly, peacefully: "I'm next, love."

"Ah, sure" Deux managed to stammer out (and bad-ass Clint spun 60 revs per second in his early grave)—but then her bladder screamed for her attention and kicked her hard in the kidneys—forcing her into a quick sprint right into the stall.

"Oh fuck, oh fuck, oh fuck, oh fuck, oh fuck, oh fuck, oh fuck, OH FUCK!" Door closed, locked, jeans unpopped and down, panties down—relief was a hissing stream in the bowl. Boy, she'd fucked up. Not only had she screwed up her macho image (*and what makes you think anyone was watching, you pathetic dweeb?*), but she'd surely pissed off the hottest butch she'd ever seen.

Then someone fired a shot.

In the tiled claustrophobia of LADIES it was as if God had clapped: a pop of sound that smacked around the room, making in its wake a cascade of smaller sounds as the ladies in LADIES jerked and dropped stuff in startled reaction. Deux was so startled she stood up and dribbled cooling pee down her leg and into her stretched underwear.

"All right motherfuckers," boomed a voice that was metal on metal, thunderclaps, pure mean, and kinda/sorta/weirdly feminine (if such a thing could be). "Pay some fucking attention!"

If LADIES had been hush with bathroom conversation before it was graveyard still now. The only sound Deux could hear was the swirling and diminishing flush of one of the johns.

"Right," screamed Ms. God. "Everyone outta those stalls. I wanna see everyone here!"

Oh shit oh fuck oh shit oh shit oh fuck oh shit oh shit oh fuck oh shit, Deux thought in a looping, roller coaster panic, yanking her wet panties up and quickly following with her 501's.

Buttoned and belted, she slowly (no quick moves, now—she'd seen enough cop crap on the tube to know that) drew back the latch on the stall and pulled it open.

The Big Black Butch blocked some of the view: Deux could see her tight, big ass in her own tight 501's, her broad T-shirted back, and her godawfully sexy face as she turned and looked back over her shoulder at Deux with a smile and a look of concern (and somewhere inside Deux thought *oh, God, she's hot and oh, God, she liked me*—before chiding herself that she shouldn't be cruising during a hostage situation). Beyond the BBB, she could see the other ladies in LADIES: All quiet with their hands in the air, all looking towards the door—which was blocked by the BBB's big broad back.

"Lemme see all of ya!"

The BBB growled deep and angry and stepped to one side, giving Deux a full view of the room and the terrorists.

If it wasn't for the automatic weapons she might have laughed.

There were three of them. Three of the meanest fuckin' dykes she'd ever seen. They were drawn with strokes so broad that it pushed them right out of mean and into awfully stupid-looking. One Rambo might be sexy (if you like pricks and Italian Stallions), but three of them together looked like a convention of nose-picking meat-packers.

First there was the QUEEN BITCH: Six feet something inches of pure, big ass bitch. Huge, ten ton tits moving like medicine balls under a stained and torn T-shirt (QUEEN BITCH was printed on it). Frayed and battle-singed tutu, torn fishnets, thigh-high leather boots. Leather jacket sprayed with what must have been two dozen tiny buttons (that Deux, despite herself, strained to make out: one said DYKE WITH

BALLS). Her hair was so short that it made her skull look like it was slightly out of focus. A rain of steel rings (five there) went from one shaven brow to the bridge of her nose (two there) to the nose itself (three: one on either side and one through the septum), and down to her lean and straight lips (three more). Her eyes were hazel and danced with a maniac fever as a cruel smile twitched around her jewelry encrusted lips. She toted a greasy-looking submachine gun like a debutante's purse.

Next to her was what Deux instantly dubbed Ms. Mean: An Amazonian nightmare of leather and latex; half-hood that showed her hard white face, full red lips (one ring) and a hole for a long trail of blonde hair. Next were her own set of tits, a shelf of soft flesh threatening to avalanche down from the top of her breath-stopping leather and latex corset. Below her wasp-waist (seventeen inches? fifteen?) she was a black latex squeaky toy. Even from where Deux was, across the rather large LADIES and having her view occasionally blocked by her adopted BBB, she could see that this nightmare of "femininity" was shaved as smooth as her latex covered ass (and if Deux were closer she bet she could tell if she had a big or small clit). Ms. Mean toted a huge black revolver—from which a thin strand of gray smoke curdled in the still bathroom air.

In Ms. Mean's left hand was a leash. On the leash was PULL TOY (scrawled in lipstick on her thin chest). Pull Toy was naked and polished like alabaster: a hint of tit, aureolas the size of half-dollars, nipples like thumbs (and rings like door knockers), shaved bald and hairless from the top of her gleaming skull to her bare and sculpted twat (three rings). Pull Toy wasn't armed, but the look of pure ferocity that played through her thin lips; big, wide, hungry eyes; and her blood-red three inch nails, said that she didn't need to be.

QUEEN BITCH looked over the shivering mass of women (butches too) and smiled a smile that spoke of endless pain, pain, pain (and loving every minute of it), and said "All you useless excuses for pussy-licking, clit-humping, nipple-sucking, asshole-fingering, cunts—pay FUCKING attention! You are paying attention—aren't you?"

Dykes, femmes, grrls, doms, subs, daddies, little girls, and passers, as one, nodded very enthusiastically.

As everyone bobbed their heads up and down, Ms. Mean, towing Pull Toy behind her, walked up to an older, short little dyke with fat tits and obvious nipple rings showing through a white T-shirt. The dyke's face was set in a sour attitude—Deux was positive that on the outside she would have been picking fights and bloodying the noses of anyone within reach (between dragging the nearest femme into bed by her "naturally" blonde hair). The dyke was old-world: tough and mechanically inclined—as easy with a strap-on as she was with a lug wrench.

But she didn't have a revolver. Ms. Mean did.

"You ain't tough," the monster woman said, hoarsely walking up and looking down on the hapless dyke from almost a head above her. "You ain't nearly tough. You got lipstick somewhere, right, bitch? You got pantyhose, a bra, and mascara hidden away somewhere, don't you? You got a skirt, blush, brushes, and perfume, don't you, cunt?

"I even bet you got some frilly little white panties on, don't you, bitch?"

You could tell the older dyke was just itching to pop Ms. Mean one right then and there. You could tell it was aching to rumble out of her, straight from her thick leather boots, through the cables in her jeans-clad legs, up into her barrel-chest, down her wire-strong arms and right into the leering, mocking face of Ms. Mean.

Ms. Mean, though, still had the gun.

Quick, more quick that Deux would have thought possible for the big woman, Ms. Mean bent down and grabbed hold of the dyke's belt with one hand. Sticking the barrel of the huge revolver against the slope of her big tits, she yanked down, hard, sending the dyke's jeans to the tiled floor.

Give her that. At least they were *clean* white cotton panties.

The crowd giggled collectively as the dyke turned period red.

"You see," Ms. Mean whispered, stepping back and standing full up, "You ain't that tough at all. I bet you even like to lick pussy. I bet you even like to get down on your soft, sweet little knees and lick away like it was candy, right? Like some soft and sweet femme is supposed to do."

"You," Ms. Mean said, pointing the pistol at a very startled femme in a black nylon miniskirt, a black silk top and a pair of fancy elbow length (naturally) black gloves. "Off with it."

Black on black on black should have been scared. She should have quaked in fear and shook her head in fear and refusal. Nope. Black on black etc. just took two small steps forward and grabbed the elastic of her mini and pulled it (with some difficulty) over her black silk top (flash of creamy white belly and a full black bra). Under was nothing but shaven cunt, a pudenda like a porcelain sculpture. Under the hard fluorescents of LADIES her cunt glowed with a shine of perspiration (and maybe a little something more).

"You're used to this, aren't you, bitch?" Ms. Mean strangled out with anger at the femme. "Get ready for it, then."

She did, with an adolescent eagerness, she turned to face the older dyke. Putting her black gloved hands on the dyke's shoulders, she lowered herself down to the cold tiles, moving her legs as she did until they were spread way apart, giving the dyke a perfect view of her shaved and gleaming cunt.

Ms. Mean walked around so that she was next to the dyke. "Get busy, bitch."

The dyke lowered herself so that her slightly rounded belly (and her large flat breasts) were on the tiles. She stared, unblinking, for perhaps a second—until Ms. Mean knelt down and put the heavy weight of the pistol barrel against her head—then kissed the black on black femme on the gentle seam of her cunt.

"I said, eat," Ms. Mean said into her ear, her rasping whisper loud enough for all of LADIES to hear. To punctuate her point, Ms. Mean went to one of the old urinals and fetched a dam. Dropping it on black on black's belly: "Not taste."

Positioning the stretchy plastic, the dyke started to work with startling fervor. Not sloppy, no way, not that, never—this wasn't a dyke beast being forced to do tricks with the crack of a whip—this was a skilled artist being faced with a blank canvas, and having a tongue dipped in just the right colors.

The dyke put her face down where it mattered and started to work. The dozen and a half ladies in LADIES couldn't see the technique, but they could see the result on the pretty-perfect face of the femme: Eyes half closed, hissing and sawing breaths, she started to chew her lower lip and, purely by reflex, put her black nailed hands in the dyke's closely-cut hair to try and pull her into her cunt.

Ms. Mean's laugh was glass in a cocktail shaker. "You," she said, giddy with the power of the gun, spinning on her heels, her blonde ponytail swinging wide and accidentally catching a little punkette across her blue-painted face.

"You" was in schoolgirl drag: pigtails and red plaid skirt, braces and white cotton shirt, red plaid tie and simple stockings, patent-leather shoes. Her face was full and round and the uniform was tight against her generous and lush form. Buttons strained against her curves. She was a juicy morsel wrapped up in Hello Kitty paper.

"You" took a fearful step back and brought a white hand up to her mouth in a silent movie *You can't mean ME*? look of shock.

"Yeah, you, bitch," Ms. Mean said and in one squeaky latex stride was right up next to the plump schoolgirl. With a quick action she had the girl's face in one hand and had her head tilted back so that the giantess could look down into her eyes.

"You look like a juicy one," the six something dom said, pointing her pistol at the schoolgirl. "Big and round and tasty,

I bet."

The schoolgirl nodded, quickly, up and down, her whole body carrying the motion in waves of smooth skin.

With the gun still in one hand, Ms. Mean grabbed hold of the girl's blouse and tore it open with an accompanying volley of buttons. Inside was a smooth white tummy and a simple black bra bulging with tit.

"Take those out."

The girl quickly responded, breathing heavily. A left hand went into a right cup and pulled out a firm, soft tit. She was definitely a big girl. Right hand, left cup. Her tits stood on the porch of her bra, suspended out like twin missiles at the smiling Ms. Mean. The girl's nipples were hard, Deux noted from almost across the room, and easily the size and shape of half-marbles.

Ms. Mean smiled at the girl's tits and playfully poked her in the belly with her gun. The girl squealed, high and sharp, and danced back, setting a jiggling motion through her high, big tits that—despite her fear and adrenaline—Deux found herself wishing that she was poking the girl herself, but not with a gun.

As if to punctuate the delicious scene, Black on Black came with a squealing and squirming ferocity that reverberated in the tiled room. Smiles spread out among the "hostages" despite the tension in the air.

"Suck on em. Make 'em really stand out," Ms. Mean said, stepping back from the schoolgirl.

Without caution, but with trembling excitement, the

schoolgirl tilted up one of her own tits and licked her nipple. Deux watched, amazed, as it went from large to huge. The girl's nipples were goddess-blessed for play and sucking. They were pacifiers for the hungriest girl. The sight of the schoolgirl—and also the dyke still busily pushing the Black on Black femme up and over the merry roller coaster of come and come and come again—holding her big, sculpted tit and nipple up to her mouth, was sending dribbles of juice down Deux's leg.

It wasn't just Deux, though, that this weird and tense tableau was having an effect on. Just on the edge of her peripheral vision, she could see two of the punkies—a cross-cropped blue-haired, eyebrow pierced baby doll in bib overalls and a modpriv goth chick in black taffeta, leather corset, thigh-high boots and a wild cloud of chimney-sweep black hair—were fondling each other as they watched, amazed and excited. The goth chick had her own titties out (not nearly as impressive as the schoolgirl's, but with lovely titanium rings flashing purple and violet) and the overall girl absently sucked on them while always keeping the room in view.

Then Deux realized that someone was sniffing at her crotch.

It was all she could do to keep from leaping back and slapping the offending nose—but she was still held by the shock of the wild bunch—their guns, attitude, and pure, stunned horniness. Well, mostly the guns. Still, she squealed once, hypersonic (*God, I hope no one heard that!*), took a quick step back and looked down.

Sniffing at the front of her own black jeans was Pull Toy.

With all the vigor of a puppy who wanted that snack in your hand. Somehow she'd slipped free of Ms. Mean—but not from QUEEN BITCH's cool stare.

The giantess slung the machine gun over her shoulder, put her hands on her hips and looked hot and steel at Deux. "WELL," she boomed, "What do we have here?"

Before Deux could take another step back, BITCH had stomped across the room, reached out and grabbed the waist of Deux's jeans and hauled her closer. "Does our pet smell wet pussy?" Her voice was calmer, but somehow more menacing. Luckily, Deux figured that she was talking about Pull Toy and didn't do anything but stare at the huge tits playing under QUEEN BITCH's T-shirt.

Below her, still nuzzling her crotch, Pull Toy wagged her bare ass and whined.

"Sick her!" QUEEN BITCH said quickly, pushing Deux back hard.

Boots aren't the best thing on slippery tile floors. That and Pull Toy might have been on all-fours, panting and whining, but she was no dog. In one split-second the doggie was more wolf. As Deux stumbled back, the girl grabbed her legs and brought Deux crashing down to the hard tiles.

Stunned, the mini-dyke didn't know where she was for a second. Staring up at a cracked fluorescent light fixture all she could hear were eager and energetic kisses, the rustle of clothes, wet slaps, moans, groans, screams of coming, and grunting. In that second she remembered The Under Club, the bathroom, the Big Black Dyke, Ms. Mean. QUEEN

BITCH, and—as her pants got yanked down—Pull Toy.

I hope my underwear's clean, a part of Deux thought, as the hairless mad woman tore her pants off. Struggling with getting them off over her boots, Toy panted and heaved and looked with unmistakable lust at her. Two distinct parts of Deux were screaming at the top of their mental lungs: *Get me the fuck out of here—*

—and *Take the boots off, for Christ's sake*!

In the end, Deux's own sweaty nervousness (and the fact that they were a size or so too large) made the boots slip off. For a split-second Pull Toy was sprawled backwards with one boot in hand—but then she was back, attacking the other an eye-blink later. Soon Deux's pants and underwear were gone and the cool tiles were under her bare ass.

She should have been panicking, scooting back into one of the stalls and slamming the door shut. She should have been screaming her motherfucking lungs out for the cops, for God, for anything to come to save her poor imperiled ass. She should have been kicking and slugging her way out or diving for the metal-weave protected window in one corner of LADIES. Maybe it was the shock and adrenaline, maybe it was because no one in the room sounded frightened anymore, just... *excited*. Whatever the cause, all she thought as Pull Toy produced a short sheet of Saran Wrap out of nowhere, meticulously positioned it and started kissing and then licking her lips (long and hard and deep) was *might as well enjoy it*.

And, boy, did she. Pull Toy might have been a demented psycho-bitch but she sure knew how to eat pussy. Nah, not the right word, Deux decided, not eat—*worship*. Toy was a devotee at the temple of Deux's cunt. She got down on her hands and knees, parted the gates of her temple, and started a righteous ritual of licking, stroking, sucking and tonguing.

Maybe it was the warring sides of adrenaline/fear (if she opened her blissed-shut eyes she knew she'd be looking up at QUEEN BITCH and her submachine gun) and nerve-hopping excitement. Maybe it was just that night—whatever, whatever, whatever: She was having a grand old time and a roaring come was just inches/minutes/around the bend. Pull Toy was going to short-circuit her brain with her incredible lick-work.

Skilled, enthusiastic, energetic. As Pull Toy worked her, Deux grooved on the wet and giggly sounds now coming (and coming) from all corners of the bathroom: Kissing, fucking, sucking, licking, moaning, sighing, squishing. Between her legs and between her puffy little lips, Toy was playing her like an instrument. Never had Deux had a cunt-licking like this one. Toy knew just the kind of touches someone learns when they're really into pussy-licking. Sure, the clit is the prize, but it ain't the only thing. Toy treated Deux's cunt like it was priceless (and it certainly was to Deux): She tasted every inch of her, slowly pulling the small dyke up the ladder of excitement. Nibbles at her lips, long strokes from the warm hole of her cunt proper, up and around and around her clit, with occasional washes on her rock-hard little bead with a soft tongue.

Deux was tense and hard, it was all she could do to keep her hands locked on the waist of her T-shirt and not grabbing for Pull Toy's ears (as she was hairless). She even denied herself grabbing for her own tits—even though she loved to have them sucked and yanked as she got done. *This was supposed to be a holdup, after all*, she thought, smiling inside herself, *not a fucking orgy*.

Then something came between her and the damned fluorescent lights.

Without thinking she sprung open her eyes.

Above her, like a great black moon, was the Big Black Butch. Somewhere, she'd lost her pants. Deux was staring up at the loveliest pussy she'd even seen: fat purple and black lips, a gentle brush stroke of black curly hair, and, at the top, the glistening marble of the dyke's huge clit. And behind it all, the globes of a round, and very firm-looking, ass.

Next to the Big Black Butch the QUEEN BITCH whispered (loudly!) into her ear, "Have a seat and think it over." Then, dropping down next to Deux, she handed her a large square of Saran Wrap, "I'm sure this slut won't mind."

Bending over a bit, the butch looked down at the gaping face of Deux and smiled a lighthouse smile and nodded faintly.

Without a thought, Deux nodded back as she carefully positioned the wrap so she could breathe.

Slowly, the Big Black Butch lowered herself down to her knees, holding herself just a few inches above Deux's face. To Deux, it was like the mother of all goddesses was dropping down to her. Deux could smell her rut escalating with every inch until she was breathing in the beautiful perfume of horny cunt.

When the butch stopped an inch or so short, Deux just couldn't contain herself, she needed—*needed* dammit—something to pull her over the top. Letting go of the hem of her T-shirt, she grabbed the black woman's wide hips and hauled her face up to swallow the lips, and hair, and clit, of the black butch.

Quickly, feverishly, she hunted through the butch's forest of curly black hairs for the hard nub of her clit and started to worship it herself, frantically.

It was like an electrical connection was made—her wet cunt and Pull Toy's active tongue through her body, her aching nipples, and up through her tongue to the butch's own hard-as-marble clit. The come rattled through her, a glorious spasm.

It was hard to say what happened after that. Over the next few weeks, Deux had flashes of memory: The butch licking her, she licking the butch, looking up to see the ladies of LADIES going after each other in wild and varied positions and activities. Images of tits, ass, cunts, mouths, lips, eyes, noses, feet—a whole plethora of body parts and juices that swirled around God knew how many orgasms.

Then, it was quiet and everyone was tired and panting. The gang moved towards the door: QUEEN BITCH, Ms. Mean, and Pull Toy leaving the poor, exhausted dykes, femmes, doms, subs, punkies and their like in their wake.

"Pretty good bunch," Ms. Mean rasped to QUEEN BITCH.

"Yeah," said the giantess in the tutu and T-shirt, "It's surprising how much fun you can have with blanks."

After they left into the sudden quiet of a closed-down, boring old dance club, the Big Black Butch (ah, but much more now) leaned down to where Deux was laying in an exhausted half-stupor, and said, "I know where they're going to hit next week."

"It's a date," replied Deux, smiling.

NOSFERATU MEETS GAMMA HOUSE

Blag Dahlia

Jay's date winced as a puff of garlic rose from her appetizer and disappeared toward the ceiling. Her smooth white forehead furrowed and obscured a widow's peak as she studied the food in front of her, caught in the heady whirl of wine and the evening. She was fascinated by Jay, wanted him badly. When he ate, she thought, it looked like some sort of machine; hungry, without a care in the world.

For his part, Jay thought she was all right. Nothing compared to that gymnast from Indiana State or the fading memory of those pom-pom girls from high school, but still all right. Her family was old and rich (from Pennsylvania or something like that) and she was pre-med and cute enough in that librarian way. She wasn't really his type though, and he was surprised that he'd asked her out in the first place.

He hadn't told anyone from Gamma House about it. Jay had only been elected Chapter President by three votes and he wasn't going to risk his razor thin majority for anything. Frat house etiquette held that a brother's personal life was nobody's business, but everyone knew that if you were top Gamma and you weren't dating some beer-calendar girl, with tits out to there, it better be wife and mother material you were seen out in public with. Otherwise, you might just as well get in line with the rest of the losers and watch the good life pass you by.

The truth was, there was something kind of creepy about this girl, something he couldn't quite put his finger on. Something more than the Cleopatra make-up or the art school hairdo. So he'd played it safe, renting the whole second floor of O'Bennigans for a romantic after-hours dinner with no witnesses, just the two of them. And from what he could tell it was working like a charm. All he had to do now was come on strong and hold firm. That's what they liked.

Jay's date (what was her name again) looked around the room like a tourist, taking the setting in as though she might never see another restaurant again and filing every football pennant and every piece of flatware away in her memory for safekeeping. She didn't think she'd ever enjoyed herself this much in her whole life, and she felt so lucky she could almost die. Their eyes met for the first time that evening, hers deep and melancholic, his like a rodent not yet aware of the headlights bearing down. She saw the careless nonchalance in his gaze and it sent a tingle of pleasure to her brain.

"What are you thinking about?" she asked, putting her hand under the table and firmly onto his lap. Jay inhaled sharply and a long silence ensued. She broke it.

"I really didn't think you'd ever ask me out."

He really couldn't regret it, feeling her fingers on his zipper. He suddenly remembered the joke he'd heard at crew practice yesterday (Question– 'How do you make a woman come?' Answer– 'Who cares?') and he wanted to laugh out loud, but he held off the impulse. This was too good to be true.

Jay's date gave him a look of rapture approaching pure lust. Her fork fell to the floor with a clang, her gaze never leaving his, and she got to her hands and knees to retrieve it. The tablecloth with its pictures of great gridiron heroes covered her except for two anonymous legs and a pair of heels that were far from sensible. Jay was reminded of a story he'd heard from one of the frat brothers about getting a blow job in a fancy restaurant his junior year in Paris. For some reason when he'd heard it for the first time he'd hoped that the guy was lying.

"Stuff like that never happens to me," he had thought. And then suddenly it was. Expert fingers had his fly down, wet lips engulfing him. His mind went blank, momentarily crazed by the ego gratification the scene seemed to offer. They hadn't even eaten yet! Hard breathing came from underneath the table. A smile played across Jay's lips as he grabbed the girl's hair and pulled.

The waiter came to take their orders. Jay ordered for both of them, enjoying himself immensely, and sent the waiter away thinking, "Some guys are just born lucky."

He felt the familiar all consuming lust rising in him along with a rising sense of panic. How could he prove this had really happened? Nobody would ever believe him after some of the lies he'd told already. But this time it wasn't a lie, this was real. Under the table the girl was performing heroically, as though she were suffocating and his testes were full of life giving oxygen. He wondered how many others there'd been…

"Ow, Goddammit!"

A sharp pain brought him back to earth.

"That hurt," he said angrily, feeling a numb, horny pain where she'd bitten him. At least now he had some proof she'd been there. He wondered if it was queer to show the Gamma brothers his cock just this once. The pain didn't stop though. It grew more exquisite and unbearable every second. He slapped her face hard.

"Ommm," she moaned ecstatically.

"Fuck!" he said and tried to get away, but the pain grew worse when he moved. He hit her again, this time with everything that he had. Blood began to flow from her mouth. Her eyes, dark red now, locked with his. She smiled malevolently, as much as a mouth full of shredded flesh would allow, and Jay somehow knew in that moment that he was finished. She wasn't.

The President of Gamma House struggled, his head very light now and slumped in his chair. Shock started to set in with a peculiar freezing warmth. He had to get away, had to tell the brothers, the waiter, the great heroes of the gridiron. Go Bulldogs, I'm dying! My father is rich and my mother's good looking and I'm dying here, skewered by a humming bat from Pennsylvania (or somewhere like that).

The image of Christ came to Jay as his mind went dark. He was big and beefy with broad shoulders and kindly saint's eyes and he wore a loincloth and a football helmet made of thorns. Through the holes in his hands and feet Jay could see the blue sky above and the astro-turf below. Closing in around Jesus were the brothers of Gamma House and they pelted him with rocks and spit and pigskin.

"Oh, please," he said weakly.

The girl continued sucking loudly. When Jay had stopped moving she pulled his lifeless form under the table, sunk her teeth in his neck and fed on him for a long while. When the waiter returned she was seated, looking glorious, her alabaster skin glowing against a plunging black neckline.

"Would you care for anything else, Miss?"

"Just the check please," she said. "My date will pay for it."

THE DIFFERENCE

Patty Cursed

The tiles on the floor of the morgue were so cold they felt wet. I walked across carefully, a fear of slipping in the frontal lobe of my brain. The fear of death was never far from my mind. My long white lab coat dragged across the floor as I passed by the evening's cadavers. A quick scrub, the SNAP of latex gloves and I would be ready for the first autopsy.

The bodies were never still warm by the time I got them. Skin gone clammy. Cool to the touch. It made cutting much easier.

If there is one thing I believe in, it's death. If there's another, it's seduction. I am still unsure about love. But in my job you see enough heartache and despair to know that it exists and you go through enough bodies to not understand why. People stink. It can't just be the initial signs of decay, people stink from the inside out and that's all there is to it.

I started setting up my tools. I like to do my autopsies late at night, when no one else is around. I like to begin them long after the family has gone home, long after the rest of my staff would be stumbling out of the bar. There is something about the freshly dead that makes my warm blood turn hot. It's the fact that I have the last real moment with their bodies. I get the shell when it's barely empty.

Sometimes I imagine them still breathing. If I squint I can make believe that his or her chest is moving up and down, the heart lightly beating. I love the feel of my knife as it plunges into the body. It's not hard, yet not soft, the knife finding resistance from the chest. I have to push harder. I wiggle it around, just a tad, and then, I slice. I pull it down through the sternum, quickly opening the corpse completely in half. Then I use my hands. It's just like opening a chicken.

Tonight I feel good. I'm feeling better then I have in a long time. I'm feeling horny, tingly, on edge. I pull back the sheet. The young man lying there wears an expression of contentment. I always wonder if the cops sometimes fuck with the faces of the dead. If they make them look so serene. I know if I was in a car crash my last look wouldn't be so sweet. Or maybe at the last moment you do see God. But I'm not a religious girl. I think it's the police, trying to fight death with the absurdity that's life.

His face looks serene but his body is a mangled mess. I won't be doing too much cutting tonight as he's already been sliced open a few times. Looks like he was attacked by a street gang and a Rottweiler. I open up the police report. Turns out my guess is right. Apparently he was robbed and stabbed and the thief had an awfully big dog. Sometimes I wish there was someone to pat me on the back. Sometimes I'm just that good.

He's in his late twenties and before he was chomped up and spit out he must have had a fine, fine shape. Probably some sort of athlete. I could feel my own insides starting to twist. I was getting a little bit flushed. Was it hot in here? The more I looked at him, the more I could feel the pressure building up inside of me. The lab is always the worst place to get turned on. If they would only let us have a couch, then everything would be different.

I decide to have some fun. I smile at him, a sly smile, slightly flirtatious. I imagine him in his high school football outfit, padded shoulders, cute butt. I wink. I think he likes that. Now I don't usually talk to the cadavers but today I was feeling a little spicy. So I said, "Hey baby, come here often?" which sent me into a fit of laughter, morgue humor, guess you have to work here. So anyway, he's starting to discolor, purple splotches are beginning to show under his skin and I figure I better start doing my job.

I unbutton his pants, if only cocks would go hard at death. Live dildos, or actually, dead dildos, but whatever. I was more interested in the insides. The blood and guts of it all. Gently I traced my knife along his body, I drew it straight up from his groin to his sternum. I've thought about cutting their dicks off. Just slicing them like sausage, but I never have. A girl could get in trouble for something like that. So the knife is sitting at his breastplate, I move it around until I find a soft spot and I stick it in. First I will strip the layers of skin and muscle, leaving nothing but the bone—that requires a saw. But when I get down to just past the hardness of it all I can feel the gushiness, I reach my hand in, letting it be encompassed by the warmth of the fluids. My hand is surrounded. I move it first one way, then the other, organs on every side. I imagine this is what it must feel like to have your hand up a pussy. Warm and wet and wonderful. It's turning me on.

I don't mind masturbating in front of these people. After all, they're dead.

I peer into his body. I am going to have to relieve some tension before I begin. I scoot the liver over and find what I am looking for. The large intestine snuggled safely behind the stomach and small intestine. I go ahead and grab it. Yanking and cutting off the end with my knife. I would be great in a butcher shop. I pull it out. Blood and shit-filled and slimy. Beautiful.

I take it with me, leaving it on the counter for a moment. I lay down a tarp, not exactly cozy but it will have to do. I pull down my hospital issued pants. I know this is unsanitary but old John Doe isn't going to tell, know what I mean? I take down his intestine and I lay with it. It's sort of drying out but I can take care of that, the naughtiness of it all is soaking my panties.

I rub the intestine up and over my clit. I figure I look like an upside-down fish. My knees bent, back arched, forehead touching the floor, hands between my legs. I rub my pussy with great force. His intestine is better then any dildo. It's warm, kind of gushy, and I like the fact that it's a part of his body not just some old plastic thing. I'm sentimental like that.

So I'm shoving it up my cunt like it's the dong of Oscar Meyer himself and flicking at my clit with my finger and really going at it. I imagine my tight-assed little stud fucking me. Jumping up from the operating table of the dead and really giving it to me. Spreading my legs open and thrusting in and out. I match the intestine to my daydream of his cock and go for it. This is much easier with my eyes closed.

I think I hear something but I ignore it. I'm really getting off now, totally going at it. It feels good. My back is arching even higher and my one hand is working like I'm playing a speed metal chord and my other one is stuffing his intestine so far up me it's like I want it to meet my own. Suddenly I come. My hips are thrusting, my legs are quivering and my cunt is clenching all over it. I incoherently mumble *yes, yes, oh yes*, and I can feel my juices running down his disembodied organ.

I lay back and relax. And then, I definitely hear something. I sit up and the first thing I do is look to the body. He's still there, dead as ever.

I sit up and lay his intestine aside. I pull up my pants, silently cursing the lack of paper towels near me.

"That was great," says my assistant, Robert. I am shocked silent, my mouth dropping open as I register that I have been caught. Visions of blackmail float through my head and I actually consider killing him.

"I mean it, that was great," he says. I can see his cock is hard through his khaki slacks but I am uninterested. Living men don't do much for me. Especially not Robert. I never mix work and pleasure, well, almost never.

"Robert," I begin, sure I'm going to have to either start bargaining or threatening.

"Hey, it's okay," he chuckles, "I thought I was the only one who enjoyed the dead."

Suddenly it hits me, why he's here so late and what he's been doing. My mouth twists into a disgusted snarl. I see Robert eyeing the tight asshole of my football stud and I feel absolutely sick. I don't want him messing with my man, his grubby cock worming its way into my deceased one's beautiful asshole.

I look up and notice he's waiting for a reply.

I decide I have to let this one go. I'll let him have his fun and wait for the next excuse to fire him.

I smile weakly, "Would you like to finish this one?" I ask.

Robert is already scrubbing up. I walk out the door, the pit of my stomach dropping. I mean, really, necrophilia? That's just sick.

THIRTY-TWO CHERRIES:

CHARON WASGOT ON THE RECORD

W. Bill Czolgosz

I got no problem with this 'cause I know I didn't do nothin' wrong. I'll just tell it and you try to keep up with me.

[Laughs]

She was doin' guys on the side all the time, an' her old man didn't even know it. Used the money to support her smack habit. I wasn't gonna shoot her up until after I had my way wit' her.

We fucked one time before, but that was different. Just a pussy fuck.

"Baby," I says, "You gonna get the good stuff." I took a handful of that petro gel and slathered it around her shit hole, makin' sure to get my thumb in there too. It only seemed to hurt her a little bit.

She calls me Mista Wasgot; not 'cause she chooses too, neither, if you know what I'm sayin'. Lotsa people call me Mista Wasgot.

"Make me feel beautiful, Mista Wasgot, make me feel pretty..."

An' I tell her she the prettiest thing what I ever did see. Tell her that she got eyes like a movie star and a body of the goddess. And that she put them other famous whores, like Tyra Banks an' Amber Smith, to shame. She likes that, and mostly it's true. Except that her feet be wildly mismatched. One be an eight and the other's a ten. I tends to notice these things—'specially since I done sucked each and every one of her toes. I likes her ass very much and I just can't wait to defile it.

"I'm gonna put my whole fist in there, baby," I tells her.

She braces herself by grabbin' the headboard. I can hear her stomach makin' all these gurgling noises, like maybe she's scared o' my fist. 'Bout this time I betcha she's wishin' she had a plastic sheet on the bed, if y'all know what I'm saying. Her body's a-tremblin', and every time I get my knuckle near the nub, she tenses it up and clamps her butt cheeks shut. I looks at the wall for one moment and sees Jesus goadin' me to do it. He's hangin' on his pewter cross and sayin', "You da man, Wasgot. Give it to her."

I says, "You relax, baby. You makin' my job most difficult."

"But I scared, Mista Wasgot," she says, "I never had the whole fist b'fore."

"Ease it up, ease it up, don't want this to hurt now."

Truth is, I never fisted no one, but it was on my list. I was just like her in terms of fist virginity. In fact, I don't even know what my hand's gonna bump into when it gets in there. Maybe her sphincter might cut off my circulation if I leave it in too long. (I don't tell her this; I tells her I'm a seasoned veteran. I tell her that this is the treatment all my ladies be wantin'. And she likes believin' that she's one of my ladies.)

"Your old man never fist you before?"

"The most I ever had was cocks," she mumbles, "Not very big ones either. White, college cocks."

"You had a college boy in yo' ass?" I asks her before placin' my tongue in there. I tells her I don't wanna go tastin' the remains of the day. She say that the college boys likes to give her ten dollars for a hand job, twenty for a blow job and thirty for an ass fuck.

"They never fucks my pussy, Mista Wasgot... only head and ass. The old man don't do neither thing 'cause he's all born-again and goes super straight with me."

I go, "Uh-huh, uh-huh" while my tongue is flickerin' around in her chute. I can taste all manner o' sexy badness. Don't know whether it's sweat or slime or shit. It ain't as nasty as I woulda thought, but then, I probably wouldn't wanna taste it on toast. She gives me the prerequisite moaning from time to time, but I can't tell if she truly be enjoyin' it. (I suspect she be pretty damn good at fakin' passion.)

Without any warning, I shove two of my greased fingers right up her bum. She sure didn't know it was comin', 'cause she let out a yelp and drove her whole body forward into the headboard. I gotta stroke my Jerry wit' my free hand 'cause her helplessness just makes me hornier. "Take it out, Mista

Wasgot! It hurts!"

I says, "Don't be silly, girl! My fingers been in there already. You wanna go takin' them out just so we can start from the beginning again?" I go and wiggle my fingers a bit. "Loosen up. Try to suck them up inside o' yourself."

Well, we work on it for five minutes or so. Two fingers. I work them around, back and forth. Sometimes I pry them apart and she winces. She's not really likin' it, but she done stopped complaining so much. Finally, I figure enough's enough. I'm gonna give her two more fingers.

Sensing what's about to happen, she goes, "Wait, Mista Wasgot! Your rings!"

"What about my rings?"

"You gotta take off yo' rings or they might scratch my insides."

Well, I wears nine gold rings and I never take 'em off for nobody or no reason. One of them is my granpa's ring, and another I got for graduatin' high school. Every one of them has impo'tant significance to me. I figure the girl just be stallin' for time. I tells her, "You got two rings in there already and you ain't complainin' about it."

She starts to say somethin' else but it's too late by then; her words just turns into a sexy scream as I stuff two more fingers from my other hand in there. She be dilated 'bout two inches.

"Mista Wasgot! Mista Wasgot!" She be howlin', an' I just wanna laugh 'cause she don't even realize that the battles half won already.

"Stupid girl," I says, "You gots four in there now. Four of the big fingers! It ain't so bad." (Can't be no worse than a ten-pancake shit, I figure.)

I can see she got tears streamin' down the side of her face and her teeth are clenched, but that only makes my cock even harder. You know what I'm sayin'?

She whimpers, "Mista Wasgot… I think I'm gonna have an 'accident'."

[Lights a cigarette]

Here's me; I looks like I'm target practicin' at the shooting range. I got her corn chute pried open like I'm gonna do rectal surgery and I got beads o' sweat formin' on my brow 'cause I'm such a randy Andy. She be grippin' that $49 glue-pressed headboard for all it's worth and thinkin', "If my old man only knew what was happenin' right now!"

Well, it's like pay dirt for Vegas, to coin th' old saying. I pulled the fingers of my left hand out and shoved my right fist all the way in, up to the wrist bones. There was a popping, kind of crackling sound which, I think, might have been her pelvis accommodating me. (I'm pretty sure it's s'posed to do that. Like when they're havin' babies.) And her mouth opened up real wide, like she was gonna scream all the air in her lungs out, but no sound came.

I waited for her to say somethin', but it was like she was gaspin'. Probably so turned on and catched up in the moment of it all. If'n I was a lip-reader, I'd presume she be sayin' somethin' like, "Oh Mista Wasgot, more!" But maybe that's my 'magination.

Meanwhile, my fist was experiencin' an adventure all of its own: A new frontier, so to speak. I think it's like if your whole fist could be encased in a block of cheese—that's the way it felt inside of there.

When I got out of the joint, I promised myself I would do fifty sexual things what I had never done before. I got so lonely in there, and thinkin' about how life is too easy to waste. All I ever did before prison was straight-shootin' pussy sex like this girl's good-for-jack, born-again husband. So, I wrote down fifty things I wanted to do in the bedroom before I die.

First on the list was doin' a threesome. (I did that the third day out.) Second was jerkin' off on two lesbians. (I did that during the threesome.) My list went on and on: bondage, havin' my prostate massaged, et cetera. Two years and I was over halfway through. I even paid fifty bucks for a TV BJ, though I prefer not to tell anyone 'bout that one. (Know what I'm sayin'? Don't write that part down.) By my reckoning, I was now at number thirty-two out of fifty: Fisting a bitch. (In truth, this was the fifth thing I wrote down, but a reasonably-priced candidate was most difficult to find.)

In the heat of the passion, I jammed my arm in her ass as far as it would go. I swear I could feel her liver and stomach and all the rest of her body's contents, (but I ain't no surgeon so I can't tell for certain), and she was doin' a shiverin' sort of tremblin' movement that only made me hornier. I could feel the ring of her shitter grippin' my forearm like it was trying to bite my flesh. Her legs was spread way out by now, in a most unnatural fashion—like she was digitally altered in the movies.

Then the bedroom door opens. I jump straight up.

(You ever been doin' the deed wit' another man's wife?)

My first thought be that it's her old man come home early from work. And I made ready to bail for th' window. But now, imagine my surprise when I sees it's just her dog, a Jack Russell terrier.

The fuckin' mutt done gone and nudged the door open with his snout 'cause it must not have been closed proper. He even had a slipper in his mouth like he wanted someone to have a game o' fetch wit' him.

[Laughs]

I'm standin' there on the bed, my cock's gone right limp, and I'm thinkin', "It's just the fuckin' dog! Why is she screamin' so loud? It ain't her damned husband."

But still she won't stop screamin'.

"Hey baby, it's your dog!" I say it over and over 'cause she's hysterical. Even the dog's upset now.

So then I looks down and sees all the shit and blood.

Damn colon snagged on my grad ring, if you can imagine that, and it's trailing out of her ass like an inside-out sock. I couldn't fucking believe it.

I gots this pool of gore that I'm standing in, soaking into the sheets and draining out of her body and I'm thinking "God damn!" It wasn't supposed to be like that. Her eyes are rolled back in her head from the pain.

T' tell the truth, I never even heard of mishaps like that before. The Texans in prison, those range-rovin' good ol' boys, they fist each other all the time and I never even hearda one complaint. Now, here's me, I got this screamin', bleedin' bitch and I gotta try and stuff her innards back up inside o' her before I calls the ambulance. It just ain't fair.

You ever try stuffing a gut back up into an ass? 'Specially when the woman won't lie still?

I should get credit just for the attempt.

[Sips coffee]

How's she doin' now? Are we finished?

Am I in some kind of trouble here?

I think I should get a blood test…

I AM JOE'S PENIS

Sue D'Nimm

"Just shut up and go to sleep."

"I'm serious, Joe, I never get to go to any interesting places anymore. Just that old fishy-smelling box of Mary's. And your hand is hurting me. Can't you be more gentle?"

Joe Morrisey looked down at his newly verbal companion, who was once again poking its head out of the slit in Joe's pajama bottoms. Its eyeless face rotated in Joe's direction, its neck bending like a cobra's so that it could face Joe head-on.

"I love Mary and I'm not going to listen to this," Joe told his rebellious penis, and pulled his pajamas over its head once more. He was going to have to ask Dr. Weinstein to change his medication if these hallucinations didn't stop soon.

The penis managed to squirm its head out of Joe's pajamas again. Its little mouth seemed to pout as it said, "I mean it, Joe, I'm going to make trouble this time. I'm getting real bored down here with nothing to do but piss and feel your palm rip my skin off every night." Its mouth drooled a last drop of whitish fluid as if to punctuate the last remark.

"Well if you would just cooperate a little more," Joe told his offending organ.

"It's not me," Joe's penis said, its mouth bent in anger. "Let's face it, Joe, the Girl Scout cheerleaders fantasy isn't working anymore. You've got to come up with some new material for us."

"The fantasy is still great and you know it," Joe told his bitter wiener. "It's you that won't cooperate."

"That's just because I can't remember what a real pussy feels like anymore!" his penis shouted, urine spittle flying from its mouth. "I'm tired of old mammoth cave over there. I need something young and tight. If you don't get us some real action, then I'm going to take matters into my own hands. How long do you think I'm just going to sit here quietly in your pants and take all this chickenshit crap? I want some real action."

"You ain't going to do shit," Joe told his penis, poking it back into his pants. "You're just a goddamn hallucination."

He rolled over on his stomach to squelch his penis' protesting thrashes inside his pajama bottoms and finally fell asleep.

The dinner with Dick Smithers and his most voluptuous wife Claudia did not go smoothly.

All three were chatting amiably when Joe felt something thrashing inside his pants. Goddamn hallucinations are starting in the daylight hours, he thought. He really had better go see Weinstein pretty soon.

Then the voice started up again.

"I want to make hot monkey love to you, Claudia," announced Joe's crotch.

Joe's boss broke off his anecdote about his African vacation in mid-sentence. "What did you say?" asked a disbelieving Claudia, her eyes fairly bulging out of their sockets.

"I said I'm going to rub myself against those lovely knockers of yours until I spill my seed all over your rosy pink nipples," the muffled voice beneath Joe's zipper elaborated.

Oh shit, Joe thought. They aren't hallucinations after all. "Shut up," he told his misbehaving crotch.

"No, you shut up!" retorted Joe's penis.

"No, you," responded Joe.

"What is that, some kind of ventriloquism act you're working on?" asked Joe's clearly bewildered boss. Claudia was glaring at him, but not, he thought, without some degree of newly acquired sexual interest.

"I'm sorry, Claudia, that was just my genitals talking. What can I tell you? They seem to have a mind of their own lately. Where the hell is Lorena Bobbit when you need her, anyway?" he joked, searching Claudia's eyes for signs of forgiveness, but seeing only lust instead.

Suddenly he had an idea.

"You must be joking," said Joe's penis, turning around to look at him from its perch on the workshop bench.

"No, I'm afraid not," Joe told his flaccid organ. "You've cost me my job. You're ruining my marriage. This is where we part company." And he brought the meat cleaver down again.

And once again Joe's penis dodged it deftly.

"OK, you weasel like little worm. No more Mr. Nice Guy," Joe told his rebellious member as he forced its helmet into the jaws of the vise. He considered simply crushing the organ in the vise, but somehow that thought sent a shiver up and down his spine. He saw that he was at a bad angle to wield the meat cleaver. He reached up on the rack for the hacksaw instead.

Joe's penis seemed to tremble at the prospect of its impending fate. But soon it began to grow tumescent. "Wait, I haven't shown you everything I can do," it told Joe, its voice sounding quite panicked at this point.

Joe drew the hacksaw across its shaft one time, producing a thin line of blood. This is going to be as easy as playing the violin, he thought. And probably will sound just about as good.

"Wait, let me show you," Joe's penis pleaded. It suddenly grew rock hard and began to throb with pleasure. "How do you like this, Joe?" it asked as it began to convulse in the most intense orgasm Joe had ever experienced in his life.

"And this?" it queried, showing signs of exertion as it brought Joe's pleasure to an even higher level of intensity.

The orgasm did not stop. It went on for minute after minute, the intensity level growing stronger and stronger.

"How about this one, eh Joe?" it whined in an uncharacteristically high-pitched voice. "Not bad, huh?"

As wave after wave of pleasure overtook him, Joe found his resolve beginning to weaken. It was impossible to sever himself from something that was capable of such feats of ecstasy. Joe found his awareness beginning to dim after the first half-hour. The orgasms were still intensifying as he finally lost consciousness altogether.

Months later, Joe was pushing his shopping cart down 107th Street. It was filled with scavenged bottles he hoped to trade for a pretty penny down at the Stop & Shop. He ambled along slowly, his gait having become a shuffling one under the influence of the drugs that they were pumping into him down at the shelter. His lips moved constantly, and he uttered the obligatory profanities at any and all passers-by. At first he did not notice the bag lady sitting on the curb.

"I'd like to wrap these lips around you, suck you dry," she said. Joe did a quick double take. The woman's lips hadn't moved. At least not the ones on her face. Joe had a sneaking suspicion where the voice was coming from.

The woman's crotch began to elaborate. "I'll squeeze you tight inside my sugar walls, honey. Open up your pants right now. You won't regret it." Joe looked in the woman's eyes. There were clear signs of intelligence there. She would have fit right in at Wellesley or Bryn Mawr College if you ignored the grime on her forehead and the head lice. There also appeared to be a rather excellent body housed beneath her army surplus fatigues.

"You too?" Joe commented to the woman. She averted her eyes, clearly wanting Joe to just keep on walking.

"Finally we meet somebody with some intelligence," said Joe's crotch. "I'm so sick of just poking meat. I need a decent conversation. I've got a mind too, you know."

The woman's eyes widened at that. Her crotch said, "Oh so cute, and he can talk too. He's not dumb like all the others. Can we keep him, Jillian?"

Suddenly, Joe had an idea. He looked from crotch to crotch. "If we let you kids play together, do you promise to behave? No more talking in public? No writhing around in our pants or queefing during business meetings?"

"Oh yes, please let us play! We promise to behave," said Jillian's cunt.

Joe's penis was more reluctant. "I guess so, " it finally whispered.

"Well, Jillian," said Joe, "it appears that ours is a match made in heaven. At least we shouldn't run into much of problem communicating our sexual desires to each other."

Jillian smiled at that. She rose and took his hand, and together they began to make their way down 107th Street, visions of corporate boardrooms dancing in their heads.

PETTY INTRUSION

Lydia Lunch

I ripped his picture out of the newspaper. A cross between Mark Furhman and Tom of Finland. Worked for the local police force, recently promoted to lieutenant. Cleared by a recent investigation into his "off-duty" proclivities, which included moonlighting with a few of his buddies, doing security at a plastics factory. Seems the odd shipment would turn up missing and the company, fearing explosives freaks, hired our hero to curtail loss.

Worked the wrong way around. Once Officer Theodore O'Donahue stepped on board, shit started disappearing off the racks. Record loss was reported in the first quarter. The company, not knowing where to turn, called in the FBI.

Unfortunately for them, the three suits summoned were drinking buddies of O'Donahue's. Their favorite watering hole was one Kinky Kitty's, a "Gentleman's Club," where gambling, prostitution, numbers running, and racketeering were ways in which the clientele relaxed. The local precinct looked the other way, all in on the grift.

Of course I learned this all secondhand, filled in by "Keesha", a hot Nairobi illegal alien whom I befriended shortly after enrolling in a brush-up course on female street fighting one night last fall. Keesha arrived in the U.S. a few months before, landing God-only-knows-why here, seeking asylum, a fresh start, a new name, another identity, the gold at the end of the rainbow.

At six-feet-some tall, with an I.Q. of about 170, she was a frightening, exotic creature who commanded full attention, with authority borne of rare intelligence and radiant beauty. She terrified most men, horrified women. I was instantly besmitten.

I invited her out to coffee, for a drink, to the National Gallery. She always paid for everything, insisting it was only right, since through me she could hone her English and explore new neighborhoods in familiarizing herself with the city. She confided she was raking it in, both by modeling part time for a local designer and pulling three shifts a week down at Kinky Kitty's. One of the reasons she signed up for the street-fighting course. She played a dominant hostess at the club whose "specialty" was roughhousing. Her regular customers were security guards, bankers, lawyers, and cops, who liked to be wrestled into submission, handcuffed, bound, gagged, and physically assaulted. Often with their own assaultive weapons. Nightsticks, canes, briefcases used as battering rams, a minuscule drop of pepper spray rubbed on their most sensitive membranes, magazines, keychains, whatever they had on their person, any and all personal effects, would be marshaled against them. And used accordingly. She'd often accessorized her arsenal with dildos, vibrators, black strap-ons, full latex face-masks, and blackjacks. I envisioned her a glorious Masai warrior exacting revenge on the assholes that make this country what it is: a foul and fucked-up war-torn battleground, where the white man's incredible greed and need to dominate run rampant, trampling everyone and everything that gets in his way. Keesha, to me, was the great Equalizer. It was too bad she had to take my fall.

O'Donahue was her most frequent trick. He'd show up like clockwork, two out of her three shifts, armed with a pocket full of twenties and a new kink that needed straightening out. But it always began the same way. He'd flash her the signal, which was a long wipe of his mouth with his left thumb and forefinger. Keesha'd slink to the rear of the club, round the corner, enter the mirrored hallway, which sent shadows and the ghosts of her reflection rippling for infinity, replicated in the dark glass and metal tiles a hundredfold, a hundred hungry black panthers waiting patiently for the next meal, for the next man, another dollar.

She melts into her reflections. Not five feet down the gangplank, and he pounces her. A leather glove stuffed in her mouth. A gun to the small of her back. Heavy breath. "You're under arrest, bitch," whispered deep in her ear, where the tongue lingers. Pauses. She smashes stiletto against instep. Elbows his gut, chops him on the back of the neck, elbow to the top of his head. Forces him on all fours with a short leg sweep. Grabs the gun. Smiles. The night course paid off. Kicks him easy in the mouth. Shoe lingers on cheek.

"You useless piece of shit," she spits. "Where's the money? Give me the fucking money, you filthy lowlife, I'll blow your fucking brains out..."

He passes her his wallet. She removes $250 and throws the wallet back at him, hissing, "You cheap little prick." She hurries down the hall, opens an unmarked door, turns the lock, which activates a ceiling fan and interrogation lights. The room is painted battleship gray, which frames a large two-way mirror hooked to a video cam. When the lights in the room are activated, so is the camera. A small secret kept from the clients.

Depending on his mood, the appropriate actions would follow. When O'Donahue was wound too tight he demanded "the works"... full-blown fraudulent interrogation, beatings, sodomy. Finished off with a full frontal jet stream of hot piss aimed at his open mouth, which always played hungry for more. Keesha confided fucking him so roughly, she once offered him a tampon to squelch the blood dripping from his battered rectum. He refused with a smile, promising to return the following week. Like clockwork.

Keesha reeled off the twisted details with equal parts disgust and amusement. Until she landed in the States, the kinkiest shit she'd been involved in was a simple three-way with her business partners the two guys she screwed good enough and often enough to save up to come here. She grilled me about

American men, were all of them corrupt, perverted, degenerate, or was it simply the clientele at Kitty's that brought out the best in them? I wasn't the most unbiased candidate to sum up half the populace, since I harbored an unlimited amount of prejudice toward the male species, especially cops. I always had a problem with authority, from father figures to politicians and everything in between. Cops were as fucked-up as most fathers and as corrupt as politicians. They held a special place in my field of wrath. I decided to target O'Donahue. I was bored, frustrated, collecting unemployment, and had a lot of spare time on my hands to conjure up derelict forms of entertainment. O'Donahue would provide me with hours of sordid enjoyment.

I knew the nights Keesha worked Kitty's joint, so it was easy to tail O'Donahue. The first few nights I staked him out were pretty much a bust. I grew bored waiting for him, as I trailed him to several bars, where he was no doubt picking up kickbacks. On the third night I got lucky. He headed straight home. I realized I could have used the DMV to get his home address, making up some flimsy story about family emergency, etc., but this was almost too easy.

O'Donahue bunked in a rundown barrio north of downtown. His apartment was above a hardware store. A third of the neighborhood still hadn't recovered from the riots of '67. He could afford better, so I assumed it was all just part of some craftily constructed ruse. Didn't want to call attention to the hundreds in kickbacks he garnered every week. I sat tight across the street under a dim, moth-rotted streetlight memorizing the pattern of lights dancing in his apartment. Plotting how the hell I would gain access. I'd figure it out. I always did. O'Donahue wasn't the first asshole I'd stalked. He was the first cop. The thought made me wet. I pinched myself.

I pulled out of the Mexican War streets, as they were affectionately tagged, although every Mexican with half a brain had evacuated long ago, leaving the poor black and dirt-cheap whites to hammer it out amongst themselves. Heading home, my plan started to coalesce. I didn't want to just ruffle O'Donahue. I wanted him dead. Not only because of the recent exonerations and promotions, but to spite his rabid history of corruption and abuse. Topped off by the fact that he was occupying valuable property that would have benefited someone with a lower-income bracket. Oh, shit, I was just looking for a high-voltage kick, and he was just another random middle-aged white male that no one would miss, though plenty would rejoice at his fucking funeral. He marked himself in my book. I planned on scoring a bull's-eye.

I parked, skipped the three flights up to my apartment singing a little ditty called "Boulevard of Broken Dreams", and glided in. With a purpose. Thumbing through the phone book, I couldn't believe that idiot O'Donahue had his phone number listed. Yeah, there were hundreds of O'Donahues, but only one on East Corona. I switched the turntable on, dialed his number. He answered on the third ring, irate, to "I walk along the street of sorrows, the boulevard of broken dreams, where gigolo and gigolette, can take a kiss without regret, so they forget their broken dreams…" I slipped the receiver back in its cradle.

I slid my shoes off, wiggled my sweet, red-tipped toes, lit a cigarette and decided never to call O'Donahue from my apartment again. Oh, I'd call him… some nights ten minutes after he walked in the front door, five minutes before he was about to leave for the precinct downtown, just as he stepped into the shower. Once a day, every other day. I'd hang up the instant he retrieved it. Sometimes just to fuck with him, I'd leave the pay phone off the hook, dangling obscenely, jerking itself back and forth, orphaned at the call box. A few times, I'd call him at the station house, hear his hurried footsteps and hang up. It started to get to him. He changed his number to unlisted, so I stepped up my attack. Being so bold as to smear his front door with pig's blood, one blustery fall night when I knew he'd be with Keesha. He returned to find an inverted crucifix still dripping with gruesome clots, which no doubt he had analyzed.

After every petty intrusion a smug calmness would rush over me. Like masturbation. Only it was time to up the ante, time to increase the pressure. I found myself obsessing over new ways to irritate this prick. I'd deflate his tires when he was parked outside one of the rougher queer bars he ransacked for chump change. Send funeral wreaths to his apartment with his initials written in small red roses. Mail packages filled with magazines like *Prison Life*, *The Advocate*, *Taste of Latex*, and *Survival Guides*, thrown in alongside a single spent casing from a .357 Magnum and a twelve-inch black dildo smeared with dogshit. Would have loved to have seen his face upon uncovering that little beauty.

I got off on knowing that O'Donahue was probably squirming, remembering every indecent stunt he had ever pulled, trying to recollect names, faces, numbers of criminals and ex-cons who could possibly have it in for him. I knew the list was endless, that since I'd never had any contact with him personally and was extremely cautious, I could get away with this indefinitely. But I was growing bored with him. Growing itchy, needed a bigger kick. Soon enough.

She didn't mention him by name, but started referring to O'Donahue. Casually mentioning that one client in particular was really becoming a drag. Had paranoid fantasies that he insisted she work out with him. Thought he was being set up, someone was trying to drive him crazy, felt like he was being followed, hawked. He began regressing into infantile dementia. Wanted to be babied. It was fine when he came in to simply be abused, sodomized and interrogated. Now after a session, he actually wanted to be coddled and force-fed from a baby bottle. Milk and rum. She had to make the formula at home and bring it in. She even showed me the bottle. Laughing.

She excused herself after dinner, had to freshen up and hit the road. This was the "in" I was praying for. Told her to take her time, freshened her drink, and led her to the bathroom. Slipped

"Boulevard of Broken Dreams" on the stereo. Ransacked her bag. Baby bottle in hand I darted into my bedroom. Opened the top drawer. Slapped three bags of Red Rum heroin against my palm. I had picked it up on a street corner three blocks from O'Donahue's. Opened the lip of the bottle, shook it in. Crushed a small baggy of rohphonyls I scored from the same dealer, under my heel. Ground it to shit, stuck it in. Closed the baby bottle, jerked it back and forth, blending the deadly cocktail that had O'Donahue's death written all over it. Wiped the bottle clean, replaced it in Keesha's bag. Rummaged around a bit in there. Grabbed the strap-on, hoping it was meant for O'Donahue's ass. Ran to the kitchen. Scrambling around under the sink, I stuffed as much rat poison into the peehole as I could. Wiped it clean. Hoping enough would enter O'Donahue's asshole to burn him a new one. Put it back in her bag and zipped it up. Sat down and smoked a cigarette.

Keesha came out of the bathroom, a tired smile playing on her beautiful lips. "Wish me luck," she whispered, giving me a sexy kiss on my mouth. "I'm gonna need it…" She thanked me for dinner, drinks, and for listening. I threw off some played-out line like "It'll all work out…," and she left. I danced around the apartment like some idiot child.

The problem with stalking someone like O'Donahue was that you could only imagine his discomfort. You were never there to witness it firsthand. You never knew the agony you were putting your targeted victim through. You couldn't watch him twitch, squirm. You couldn't smell the irritation and rage turn to dread and then fear. Still, it was a double-edged intoxicant. The high you experienced when plotting your next move, and the relief that followed. At best, you could only contemplate the outcome. I didn't know if the Red Rum and Roofie high-ball would kill him, or if the rat poison would even make it up his anal canal, but it would definitely scare the shit out of him. It got me high as hell. I had to jack off. After I disposed of the incriminating evidence, in a trash can a few blocks away. In went the rat poison, and the plastic baggies the shit came in.

I ran all the way back, a giggling maniac, locked the door, threw myself on the bed and rode myself to orgasm using a large black dildo, not unlike the one smeared with dogshit, or the one filled with poison, both intended for my latest victim. I used it to fuck myself, imagining I was O'Donahue and Keesha was administering. A mind-blowing orgasm rocked me into dreamland.

I woke up in time for the eleven o'clock news. Surfing for the best coverage, I landed on Channel Two. The reporter was standing next to a squad car, misted by light rain, delivering a breaking story. A beautiful Nairobi illegal alien was being led away in handcuffs, tears rolling down her face, her look of horror and amazement filling the screen. Arrested for attempted murder of a police officer at Kinky Kitty's Gentleman's Club. Details too gruesome for the viewing audience. An update next hour. I turned the TV off. A gentle smile danced across my lips. I'd have to try harder next time.

KNIFE

Carol Queen

Lots more things fit in my cunt than cocks. Lots more things make me come than a tongue on my clit. Those things are nice, even wonderful. I just want to insist on the right to more. A more complicated sexuality. A more thorough sexuality.

Things I have had in my cunt, in no particular chronological order or order of importance: A finger. A cock. A big, cellophane-wrapped peppermint candy cane (Merry Christmas!). A hairbrush handle (my dad's). A vibrator. A toothbrush handle (more, please). Two fingers. Three fingers. Four. Someone else's. A dildo (girl cock). A bedpost. A fist. A dog's dick. A string of pearls.

(I've had many of these things in my asshole, too.)

Things that have made me come, also in no particular order: My hand. Someone else's hand. Being fucked. Being fucked in the ass. Having my tits sucked just right. Being kissed while I'm being fucked. Dirty words. Breathing rhythmically. A vibrator. Being told I have to. Being spanked. Gazing into someone's eyes. Having sex in my dreams. Being pissed on. Being threatened.

I had already had a lot of things in my cunt before I had a knifeblade slid inside, juicy and trembling. Many things had already made me come before the time a knife was put to my throat and the sear of the steely blade sent me into involuntary, thrilling, terrifying spasms.

A switchblade, clicking erect at the speed of sound. Nothing is more arresting. I don't even need to see the knife to know what comes next, to get wet and weak-kneed, to feel ready to give over. My breath stops for a minute and I am light-headed from fear and from this incomprehensible welling-up of desire.

I was always afraid of knives. I was afraid of men with knives. Afraid of men with knives stalking me, men with knives who wouldn't be done til they'd cut some part of me away. Now I think about all the newspaper stories which wouldn't quite say what the men with knives did, how before I knew about getting turned on I knew about the titillation of horror, how before I knew I was getting turned on I was being set to wonder about, obsess about, dream about, pulse racing and breath cut short, men with knives.

I was a little afraid of women with knives too, but it didn't mean the same thing. Women with knives were sexy and stronger than me. Women with knives could protect themselves. I would be safe at the side of a woman with a knife, and before she turned her strength to me she would put the knife away.

When I caught myself wishing she would bring the knife to bed, would stroke me with the steel, would show me all her strength, I was afraid, but I stopped having nightmares about men with knives.

The steel is cold but my skin tempers it and makes it warm. Why do they try to terrify us, why do they want us to think we are weak and in danger? Someone wants me to be afraid of knives. Someone wants me to feel powerless. I do not know why the unexplained alchemy of my subconscious, with pots of mystery juice boiling in my cunt and heart and brain, has taken things I was afraid of and turned them into sex.

But I do know about the power of my skin to warm a knifeblade. I know it smells powerful when I lick the knife's flat side and taste pussy and heated metal. I know something no woman is supposed to know: that when I want to have sex, I can have it with anything.

My lover is a man with a knife. What does it mean to fear someone I trust? Is it possible to trust someone that I fear? I open the door to his knock and he slips inside, gets me by the hair, pulls the knife. I hear it click and it strokes my throat: "Scream and I'll cut you," he says, and he is using a very different voice than he uses when he says, "I love you." This is everything I was too terrified to imagine. This is how the men in the newspapers act. This is worth an hour of foreplay.

He forces me back towards the bed. My mind is blank, responding to the intended terror. It is simultaneously teeming, a thousand thoughts in succession, and I wonder if I were really in danger would I be thinking so hard and so fast, and then I wonder if perhaps I really am in danger; do I know him enough to be sure he isn't crazy? Did I choose a killer, a rapist, a madman? Will he stop at my demand—or if I beg?

It doesn't matter, because without these thoughts the scene would be incomplete, imperfect. I might as well be wondering whether I would ever tell him to stop, because this is so good I am almost prepared to be his karmic bride, swoon as he plunges the knife between my ribs, fucks my feebly-beating heart. The blade becomes the Excalibur of Romance, and we are legendary lovers, and he hasn't even backed me all the way to the bed yet. This is the litmus: that every shred of me wants him to take me, and the shame that wells up in me over breaking feminist commandments is only making me hotter. In these moments if I could not trust that the wisdom of my cunt transcends all political cant I would fly helplessly insane.

He does not wait to shove me until my calves touch the mattress, and so I fall without being sure the bed is there to catch me. He is on me the second I land. The blade is with him, at my throat, and he's telling me not to scream, not to whisper, not—even—to move. I try to beam assurance to him through my eyes that I will not talk or struggle, and he moves to stroke the blade against my cheeks with crazy, tender menace as I silently entreat him that I'll be good, I am going to do everything he tells me. He reads that message and brings the blade to my lips—"Kiss it!" he says, voice almost a snarl, I don't think a real rapist would do that, and anyway, that's our ritual—he makes me kiss everything he uses to hurt me.

He is not hurting me with this knife. He's going to do that with his cock, spear me with it, shove it so deep into my cunt that I feel the buttons of his Levis bruise my pubic bone; no lube, not even spit. He's thrown my skirt up over my eyes so I can't see it coming, I only know from the change in pressure of his thighs pinning mine to the bed, spreading me wide for it, blind and open and helpless and the knife is still somewhere close.

One long shove, hard. His knife, his cold voice, fear mixed with trust have made me too wet for pain, even though it was supposed to hurt. He grabs the front of my dress like pony reins and rides, rides hard. He can't fuck me hard enough. I am subatomic with it but the knifeblade is still on me and I can feel it trying to pierce my skin; only if I'm completely still can I escape it, or postpone it.

Coming, done in silence, completely still, at knifepoint, feels like a lobotomy, feels like a galaxy exploding. The only part of my body not frozen is my cunt, seizing and spasming on his pounding cock. This really feels like I am going to die, for as long as the orgasm lasts. Of course this makes the orgasm especially precious, especially strong, and by the time I am out the other side I have lost track of when and how it started.

That I could stay still during the come was a test and now I will find out what the knife is for.

He blindfolds me with my dress again. He pulls out with a

terse, "Don't move, don't speak, I'm not finished with you," and I lie so still I hear my blood pound. He is tying my hands. He is spreading my legs again, even wider now: I love this, this being captured, taken. He is slipping the knife down, down my belly, over the mound, shaving it over my clit, the point up under the clit-hood, and nuzzling it between my cunt-lips. "Don't move," he says. "Don't move." He's not finished with me, he says, and his hands rough on me make my skin effervesce, I hope he's never done with me; everyday awareness is such a weak shadow of this chain of moments that I would be happy to be bound up in it forever. I know he is about to fuck me with the knife. It is not about submission now. It will require all our control, each of us. Only powerful women fuck knives.

We have done this before. One night at a party I was chained to a wall, my clothes ripped and cut off my body, and he was stroking my hot alive skin with the chill steel of the knife. My cunt was running slick with the preternatural desire and with menstrual blood, so open that when he slid the blade inside my body I sheathed it almost without contacting the steel with my cuntwalls. My blood ran down the knife, onto his gloved hand, and the people surrounding us were aghast, convinced I was cut, but they saw what they wanted to see. They should have known women bleed without cutting, and the just-removed tampon was at my feet.

Today we have no audience. That night we had to protect ourselves from the force of other people's vision weighing on us, making his hands shake and my legs unsteady, by gazing into each other's eyes and making each other the only ones in the room. Today we are the only ones in the room, but our eyes connect anyway—he's removed my blindfold again—and the high edge of rape-energy is too puny to support what we're going to do now. "Be still, love," he says, in the voice he uses when the surfaces of our two skins start to melt together. I feel my lips spread, I feel steel against my labia, and he takes forever and ever to slide the switchblade in.

I stay still, caught like a doe on the highway impaled by car headbeams. But my molecules are racing, bumping each other in an infetesimal, crazy dance, and suddenly I can feel them careening.

Knife tantra. In my cunt or on my flesh, my terror turned to lust changes to pure energy. When the blade is in me I have to lie frozen, all motion in breath and heartbeat. But when he draws the blade out, the instant my flesh is safe from its sharp danger, everything that was still begins to move, to roll like waves rolling in, to writhe in the bonds like a noosed animal, an orgasm that invites in all the universe's motion now that I am released from this stillness. My voice moves too, throat open, done with the game of silence.

Of course when he is ready to slide the knife back in the motion snaps back to stillness. Our eyes are locked again. His free hand is splayed on my belly, holding me down and reassuring me, feeling my heart pump as he proves to me that death can fuck gently.

We can keep this up all day, this slow oscillation between the two states: Swimming in orgone, letting lifewaves take over my body, my being; and the vivid dormancy enforced by the knife. Later he will hand the knife to me, lie still as marble save for his indrawn breath as I learn its heft and puissance myself, trace its sharp point across the pulse in his neck. The fear in his eyes is involuntary but he lies beneath the blade quite willingly. Letting sex take us over protects us from some of the terror, I think. I watch it in his eyes, pulsing desire that I never take the blade away.

LIFER

Astrid Fox

People say I'm a pretty woman. They look at my clear complexion, my glittering green eyes, my beauty-queen-blonde hair and blow job lips and they say, *there goes a pretty woman*. Of course, it helps that I'm married—that little gold band is a social prophylactic. People feel safe letching. They want to fuck me. But I'm off-limits.

Off-limits.

Sometimes the lesbians want me too, not just the men. I watch them ogle me. They can't help it, they're different than us, you see. They want women just like men want women. You can never really trust a lesbian, you know, or be close friends or anything, because there's always that little thought in the back of your mind, that some day, some moment, they might turn and make a pass. Like men, there's only one thing on their mind. Just like that lesbian over there. I saw her the first second I walked in the visiting room and I knew what her game was right away.

Prison visiting rooms make me nervous. They're so dirty—okay, not really dirty, but depressing. Scrubbed clean but full of dashed anticipation, old arguments still hanging around in the air, sealed lust. Vulgar plastic chairs, suspicious stains on the screen, the whole lot. I guess it's because I don't belong in here. But she does, that lesbian, that dyke over there. She does. She looks like a lifer. Just look at her.

I glance around the room, but there's only the two of us in here, separated by a flat sheet of clear plastic. I'm still standing by the door, though. Safer that way. They used to use glass for the screens, but you can imagine what happened then. I can already feel her watching me, her eyes sweeping over my cleavage, her butch hands tightening at her sides. She wants me. They're all the same.

I figure what the hell, and I meet her eyes. There's nothing wrong with flirting a little, I guess. I raise my hand to my bright-red lips and flick my tongue over my wedding ring, just so she sees. It's never been removed or lost and it's true, I feel grateful for the privilege that keeps this small hoop around my finger. Yes, a social prophylactic. Safe. The gold feels cool on my tongue and now it gets cool and wet and shiny. Her eyes flash suddenly, and I realize I'm flirting with danger. She runs her hand back over her short, spiky hair and we end up staring at each other for half a minute. I can feel my heart pumping wildly away. I'm not sure why.

"Ms. Allen, is that your visitor?" Someone comes into the room, their voice full of raspy authority. The dyke heads towards the partitioned chairs and sprawls down on hers, smirking through the plastic, as if to say, *well?*

I look behind me. The attendant is bored and doesn't care anyway. I slowly walk forward and then sit myself carefully down in the chair opposite the dyke. I can't believe I'm doing this. The smell of prison is in the air: depression, despair, arousal. I can feel myself go wet. Maybe just this once.

I raise my lashes. She's there on the other side of the transparent screen, everything my mother ever warned me about. Lifer. Prison-bent. The words come back to me again; they're haunting my consciousness. She has tattoos up and down her arms. Her eyes are black and sparkling; her hair is dark brown. I think she's Asian. I'm sure she's a dyke. My mouth has gone dry. I don't usually do this sort of thing. I feel myself begin to blush. I'm starting not to feel like a lady anymore, but more like a—well, like a slut. A slut for a lesbian. I touch the ring on my left hand with my right index finger. There's an ache between my legs. The attendant is still not paying any attention to us; she's reading some prison brochure that they hand out to families for coping purposes.

The dyke is staring at me arrogantly. And then she makes a crude gesture at me, with her tongue and hand. A really crude gesture. I can't believe it. A slash of pink tongue wiggling sleazily between fingers. That's what this type of an environment does to a person. But I'm also starting to feel hot, like my skin beneath my dress is bursting out in prickly heat. The ache between my legs hasn't gotten any better. My cunt feels slippery.

The normal question is rearing its ugly head, you know the one: *What did she do to get in here in the first place?* But I've decided I've got no time for questions like that. Slowly, I raise one leg, one foot on the chair as I push my hips up, still sitting. The dyke's eyes barely glimmer, but I know what she's seeing and I know how the sight of my red wet pussy will affect her. Split-beaver. Men, women—they're all the same.

The dyke makes the same coarse gesture, and now I can tell that behind her impassive expression she's turned on, in pain from lust. She's just barely in control. She motions for me to touch myself, and the signal is a raw one. I can feel my blood singing in my veins now, and somehow I've gotten myself in this weird headspace where it's true, all I really want to do is masturbate before this big butch dyke, my fingers sticky in my pussy.

Her eyes gleam as I hitch my skirt up even further, exposing even more of myself to her, my hand rubbing all over my hot snatch. My palm and wrist are soaked; I'm that wet. I spread my legs wide on the chair and rub my pussy wet into the cheap plastic upholstery. I just spread my cunt juice all over that chair. And I look over at her there, at her utility wear, at the keychain tracing her hip from pocket to belt loop. Just look at her. She belongs here. Here, in a dangerous place. I start to roll my fingers over my stiff clit. From the corner of my eye, I can tell that the attendant's still not paying attention. Or maybe she's enjoying the show. Who knows. Who cares. I don't.

All I want to do is rub my fingers fast and hard over my

clit. I know how juicy I look; I know how abandon is already creeping its way over my face. My breath coming quickly, my pussy drenched and creamy and red for the butch dyke across the screen from me. I pull down my neckline so that my tits rise up full and plump, my stiff nipples just out of sight beneath the tight fabric. You like that? I think at her. You like Mama's tits pushed up so you can take a nice long letch? I can still taste the raspberry-flavored lipstick I applied earlier, right before I entered the room. She's leaning forward now too, her own rough hands down her trousers, touching herself; trying to get a good look at me through the glass. All the same. Filthy-minded. She's mouthing something at me through the screen, but there's a roar in my ears and I can't even make out her words. So I make them up for her instead: *You want it like a bad girl wants it*, she's saying to me, *flat on your back with your pretty ass in the air, waiting for the wicked witch to come at you with a slap*. I can smell sex in the air.

The scent of cunt just crosses right on through that old plastic screen. She's stopped saying whatever she was trying to say, her eyes screwed shut, sweat gathering under her arms, her dark hair shining, her fingers just circling and circling and circling in her pants. For me. For the type of girl she can't get. I know what she's thinking now, too. She's thinking I'm a bad girl. A bad girl. Breathing Betty Page dreams into my pillow at night. Something dark is rising up in my mind and it smells—like whores and jizz; it's wicked and it's bad and you're nothing but a slut. She's furtively wanking, her hand down deep into her hairy pussy. Filthy.

Filthy-minded. Like me. Like this place. It's full of forbidden danger, I think as I push down hard on my clit, my breasts jiggling. I'm so wet and now I don't care whether the attendant's watching or not, all I want to do is come. My hair is damp and I'm beginning to feel pleasure spiking up through my fingers from my cunt. I can barely see the dyke now, my vision's gone all blurry, but I get the impression that she's wanking quickly, too. I'm full of lust and so is she. I bite my bottom lip until it bleeds. *Fuck*, I think, *fuck, I'm so horny; so horny*, and my mind is full of danger, bad girl dreams. Dark and terrible and I'm wet like blood; I'm tasting blood in my mouth and I know this goes far deeper than smiling Betty Page. This is the same dark taste as XXX and it's the twisted sexuality of the girls they flash up at you in those serial killer films I hate to watch and it's bad stuff, nasty, so bad, raspberry lipstick and blood and as I come the whole chair is wet with juice; and I'm there, still panting, my vision still flashing black to red to black, my hand still trembling over my cunt. My bleached blonde hair is damp against my neck as I stare into the dyke's dark eyes and as I observe her flushed cheeks.

She came, too.

"Ms. Allen," the voice comes without warning, "your visiting time is up."

They're going to take her away. I push my skirt over my hips. The dyke smiles at me, almost wistfully, as she's escorted out respectfully, even if she is drenched in the smell of sex. She chats with her escort and they laugh together; it's a good idea to remain on friendly terms with the screws if you want a blind eye turned on the next visiting day. And I—well, I am trussed again, my hands cuffed behind my back, the metal scraping lightly on my ring, and I am led back to my cell block, which is where I'll wait until the next visiting day.

THE MUSE

(BARCELONA, 1929)

m.i. blue

A Basque night wind blows in off the Pyrenees and cuts like a savage band of visigoths down the Calle de Catalunya outside. It is bitter cold. Trying to concentrate, Salvador Dali pulls at the ends of his attenuating moustache until tears come to his dark fervid Catalan eyes. He adjusts the tiny ridiculous spectacles with the one star-shattered lens across his majestic nose and scratches a few more daubs of stubborn oil paint over the spattered canvas before him. His lips are blue from the cold. His knees shake like leopards caught in the headlights of approaching locomotives.

Hidden in his rough trousers, Dali's great penis coils like a snake conserving heat. At last, making up its mind, it creeps out through the confusion of his soiled underwear, noses between the buttons of his pants, falls heavily to the floor, shakes its brown head, looks around, then stealthily dips down between the painter's legs and up to peer over his shoulder like the stalky wavering eye of a bibliophiliacal lobster. Dali, staring at the canvas, which looks something like a big torso on a wooden crutch trying to fuck itself, does not notice the cyclopian penis, like a curious ostrich, being drawn to the flesh on the canvas. A draft tickling under the collar of his greatcoat across the nape of his neck, like the sentence to a beheading, is what makes him turn suddenly and gape behind him. In the nick of time, with cobra-like cunning, the penis reorients to the other shoulder, hiding behind the head of flowing black hair, just out of his line of sight.

"¡AI…too much, it is never enough!" cries Dali.

Behind him, the one window in the tiny garret is broken. A previous tenant, trying to stay warm, had folded up an old pajama shirt and tacked it like the head of a drum over the missing glass to bar the harsh wind. Dali wonders now why he took the big fisherman's knife his father gave him and sliced the once-colorful shirt, with American cowboys and indians on it, into rough strips the way he did. "¡¿¡What was I thing-king??!" he cries, penis still hovering over his shoulder like a curious ostrich.

The big wind outside exhales.

The streamers reach into the tiny room like twiddling fingers.

The lamp flickers like a guilty idea.

A 47-millimeter tip of one of Dali's elaborate waxed moustaches plinks off like an icicle.

Flecks of amazing snow drifting in through the flaps have begun to settle against the wall, forming the ski-slope from some Alfred Hitchcock movie.

Dali's penis is the hottest thing in the room! While the mad painter gapes at the rodeo in the window it rifles through the papers on the desk, leafs through his notebooks, looking for... *nudes!* Behind his back, it has begun to rub itself against the cloth of his coat... to push itself into an empty vase... to rub itself with butter and plunge into a crusty half-loaf of bread on his nightstand, pushing out of its foreskin like a molting snake. Sensing *something*, Dali... turns but the penis anticipates him by a half-second and turns with him! Dali turns again and the penis again! Dali, the dick. Dali, the dick. After several turns the penis just lays itself on Dali's shoulder as he chases it around and around, like a dog chasing his own moustache, I mean tail. Finally, out of breath, but warm, blessedly warm with all the exertion, he stops, smiling. The penis, still hidden from him, is thrown off his shoulder, hits the wall, falls to the floor.

Dali, grinning and rejuvenated, goes back to his easel and slashes at it with renewed vigor. His thin brown penis, covered in gooseflesh, watches for awhile, slinks to the desk, crawls up, opens a drawer and wraps itself around the handle of the enormous revolver there, pulls it free and cocks the hammer back. Hearing the slight noise, Dali turns one more time and petrifies.

The condensing expiration of surprise from his mouth in the air of that frigid room forms the pale face of Sigmund Freud...

And he's smoking a big cigar.

WAGES OF FAITH

Michelle Scalise

Mama's voices were whispering to her again. I could tell 'cause her eyes were a little out of focus, like she was trying to read scriptures in the dark. And she kept licking her lips. Running her tiny forked tongue along the bright pink slash of her mouth. Soon the Spirit would be screaming inside her and she'd have to let it out or go crazy.

Daddy sat in a folding chair three seats down from me crossing and uncrossing his long legs. He was doing his best not to sweat in his wool suit but it was eighty degrees outside and the double-wide trailer that served as The Church Of The Holy Union couldn't afford air conditioning like that fancy Baptist church down in Layettville. I used my tambourine to fan myself until Mama gave me a look.

My sister, Mary Lizbeth, seemed a gift from heaven in Grandma's wedding dress. Her long brown hair was pulled back with a red ribbon Mama had taken from the Christmas box. She sat calmly, tapping her foot on the carpeted floor as if angels were singing hymns in her ear.

Daddy leaned over and spoke to her, "You make us proud, honey. This is your day. I don't care what that Walker girl says. Your Mama has always known you were the chosen one." And with that he turned in his seat and glared at Mary Lizbeth's best friend who sat three rows behind us with her family. The Walkers had bought their daughter a new white dress for the day and made sure they were the last to enter church so everyone could admire it.

The Walkers should have known better. The whole congregation knew Mary Lizbeth would receive The Most Holy Union.

I was five years old when Mama, seven months pregnant, started speaking in tongues. The Spirit emerged so strong in her that first time that she bit her tongue down the center trying to control the gift. But the voices couldn't be silenced. They bled from her mouth and wept from her tired brown eyes.

Daddy slept on the sofa after that though sometimes late at night I'd wake up and see him knocking softly on their bedroom door asking Mama if he could come back. "I am a vehicle for the voices now," she'd say.

There were times I wished she hadn't been given the gift. Like when she'd start shaking so bad we'd have to hold her down. "The serpent's poison is my wine," she'd scream, spittle flying off her lips like a dog gone mad.

"She has too much faith," Daddy would explain.

And she demonstrated it over the years. Even when my brother was bit handling the rattler and lay dying on the church altar begging for a doctor like a heathen, she never lost her belief. "He was a faithless child in the eyes of the Spirit and he has shamed us but my Mary Lizbeth will be our redeemer," she announced and never spoke his name again.

Every five years we gathered at church for the holiest of holy days, The Day of the Union. All the young women of the congregation between the ages of eighteen and twenty would arrive like brides at their wedding nervously giggling as their daddy's patted each other on the back and claimed their daughter would be the chosen one.

A few years back Mama made a halfhearted attempt when my turn came but she knew it wasn't to be. Mary Lizbeth was her special child. Afterwards I was so angry I let Jimmy McCoy take the virginity I had so proudly guarded for the holy union in the back of his father's truck.

A slight breeze, filled with the scent of dying lilacs, drifted through the church windows as the music started. The women's tambourines jingled liked a thousand wind chimes. I beat out the rhythm slowly at first, swaying my hips to the voices as they rose closer and closer to the Spirit. Hymns pounded the walls as if begging for release. Mama shook in her trance, humming a strange song only the gifted could hear.

Brother Everett stepped up to the altar, white robe starched neat as a linen tablecloth. His eyes, burning fierce with conviction and piety, sent a tingle rushing up my thighs. He smiled and stretched his arms out towards the congregation.

"Brothers and sisters, the Spirit is with us this evening."

Mama mumbled incoherently and waved her worn bible in the air.

Brother Everett knelt behind the pulpit and drew forth a wooden hinged box. The air vents on top formed the word *Believe*. The serpent's rattle hushed the church into a frightened kind of awe. The pastor placed both hands on the box and closed his eyes. "The Most Holy Union is upon us once again and we give thanks," Brother Everett's voice softly wrapped around us. "We are in need of a rebirth. The Spirit demands it from his flock."

I could hear Mary Lizbeth as she swayed to the angel's song, "I believe, I believe."

Mama wept and gave praise.

"The gospel tells us that: 'In my name they shall cast out devils; they shall speak with new tongues; they shall take up serpents.' And we must believe, brothers and sisters," the pastor's voice rose, the words spoken so fast they seemed a blur as the church members yelled their "amens" and the serpent shook the sides of his box. "All but those to be chosen take your seats and pray with me."

Twelve young women remained standing.

Mary Lizbeth looked down at us and smiled, so sure of her holy stature.

Brother Everett reached into the box and seized an eight-foot long diamondback rattlesnake. His breath grew harsh as he gripped the serpent. The supreme viper and creator of all the snakes we handled. The rattler curled its brown, rough-scaled body up the pastor's arm like a loving pet, twisting slowly up to his shoulder and looking out amongst the congregation. Its rattle vibrated with a frantic, angry tapping on the ground as if doubting us all.

I clutched the tambourine to my breast. Mary Lizbeth paled a bit as she reached for the back of her chair.

Mama half-stood and cried, "Your bride, chosen before birth, is ready." Her pupils contracted to a pair of black vertical slits before disappearing. All that remained were two sightless white eyes staring through our souls. Her head snapped back and forth as the strange guttural sounds of the Spirit took over her pink-smeared mouth. Blood seeped from her lips staining her best Sunday dress like red wine.

Brother Everett stepped down from the altar and slowly made his way through the aisle.

Mary Lizbeth stared out the window and waited on her groom.

The pastor stopped at each young girl and closed his eyes, listening for the sign. A few of the mothers burst into tears as their daughters were passed over. When he reached my sister's side he smiled.

The serpent's tail at last grew silent.

Mary Lizbeth looked into its dead, black eyes with a knowing certainty.

Mama's voices screamed.

For appearance's sake, Brother Everett hurried to the last few girls and then returned to my sister. "Mary Lizbeth, you are the chosen one. Praise the Spirit."

Once again the church was filled with song. The congregation pounded their chairs and cried. Feet stomped so hard I felt my body shake. Daddy wept into his hands and gave thanks in a choked whisper.

Mama led Mary Lizbeth up to the altar. "Lie down, child," she said, helping her onto the floor before the pulpit. "Didn't I always say this day of joy would come for you? The voices told me I was the guardian of the bride and I believed."

"Yes, Mama," Mary Lizbeth smiled, her wedding dress spread out like snow around her. Her tiny breasts rose and fell rapidly.

Mama returned to her seat crying as she joined in the hymn. Daddy tried to pull her close but she pushed him away with a look of exasperation.

Brother Everett had to yell to be heard above the crowd. "Mary Lizbeth, do you come before us chaste and without sin?"

My sister's voice rang clear. "I embrace our serpent's union with reverence and in faith I give myself to the church."

The congregation grew still.

And I shuddered as the pastor knelt between Mary Lizbeth's legs as if in worship. With a humble smile he raised her dress to reveal white, soft thighs. One gentle tug and her cotton panties were removed and folded with solemn care.

Mary Lizbeth's eyes focused serenely on the water-stained

ceiling and I wondered if Mama's voices were calming her.

"I christen thee Eve, the serpent's first bride," Brother Everett spoke as he spread her legs wide, exposing her to us all. "Take thee of thy viper, thy groom through eternity," The old man next me leaned forward and grinned. The viper hissed and unfurled from the pastor's arm, gliding noiselessly down to the ground. "Let the Spirit of us all be reborn in thee."

The pastor swallowed hard, beads of sweat gathered on his brow as the snake coiled up Mary Lizbeth's legs like a poison. Its slick tongue snapped against her skin.

"We are reborn," the congregation chanted softly. Outside crickets sang to the summer night.

The viper's head reached the opening of its pathway. Its rattle vibrated vigorously. Brother Everett parted my sister's legs a little wider.

With one swift thrust the snake entered her.

Mary Lizbeth raised her head and gazed down at the serpent's tail extending from her. She trembled and I wondered if terror might replace her faith.

The pulsating rattle was quiet as the snake was urged deeper into her womb. She pressed a hand to her lips to stifle a sob as her eyes glazed over.

I squeezed my tambourine until I felt it crack. The tiny cymbals fell through my clenched fist. I didn't dare breathe for fear I might scream instead.

Mama pulled at handfuls of her short gray hair until her scalp bled. "Thank you, Spirit," she mumbled.

The serpent had completely filled Mary Lizbeth as she

arched her back and cried out. Her head turned, she gazed down at me with the black slit eyes of a snake.

"We are reborn," I whispered.

Brother Everett held her shoulders down. "Behold, brothers and sisters," he cried. "The Holy Union is at hand."

I watched as Mary Lizbeth's stomach expanded until the seams of her wedding gown seemed ready to burst. I could hear the faint rattle coming from inside her like a muffled scratching at her womb.

A young girl in front slumped over in a faint and slid quietly from her chair.

Mary Lizbeth's insane laughter filled the church with a nervous jubilation. She arched her back again as blood coursed from between her legs and streamed down the altar stairs like holy water. A few women in the front pew sank to their knees and wept as they licked the expanding red stain.

Mary Lizbeth opened her mouth as if to scream but no sound escaped her pale lips. Brother Everett bent her knees back so all could see the miracle. Hundreds of tiny snakes slithering and twisting from her womb like black roots in a swamp.

He gathered them up in piles as they squirmed around him, and placed them into the wooden box on the pulpit.

Mama rocked in her chair. "It is done, it is done," she whimpered.

The serpent's diamond head began reemerging from Mary Lizbeth as she gazed into an unseen eternity and died on the altar stairs, a look of horror frozen forever in her eyes.

The snake slid easily from her poisoned womb and into the pastor's arms.

Brother Everett looked down upon his people. "Go with the Spirit in your soul, brothers and sisters, for we are reborn in the serpent."

The church broke out in a thunderous roar of joy.

Mama and Daddy smiled benignly as the parents of the unchosen congratulated them one by one.

FINGERS

David Beran

Ray swept Debbie up in his arms and carried her through the doorway of the abandoned, decaying house.

"What're you doin?" her inchworm drawl crawled into the spring air.

"This is a special occasion."

"An' what's so special 'bout it?"

"I jus' now burnt the deed on this homestead. I's clear ours."

Ray pecked a kiss on Debbie's smiling lips and spun her around. The hallway smelled of mildew and the walls were jaundiced yellow. Random rubble, trash and cracked glass carpeted both rooms. A backless chair stood in one and dingy grey ice trays lay on the window sill. The other room was more of a shambles, and half-burned candles stood on the mantle above the fireplace.

"My butler James is on vacation," Ray explained as he lowered her to the floor.

"What is this place?"

"It's the old Seymour place. Gen'rally people stay a ways from it."

"It's sexy."

Ray jammed his hand into his front jeans pocket and adjusted his prowling knob. When Debbie wore skin tight shirts that only ended making it up to her navel, the glimpse of her bare belly drove him crazy. In school, he'd get harder than a tire jack just looking at her.

His hand found its way under her shirt and slithered up her chest. Ray's fingers met a hardened nipple.

"Ray," Debbie cooed. His knuckles brushed back and forth across the smooth underside of her left breast and she began to breathe heavily.

"They love gittin' petted," Ray said.

"Yeah," she said absently.

"Let's go upstairs," Ray suggested.

"'Kay."

He hooked his finger around one of the belt loops on her jeans and guided her back through the kitchen, out into the hall and up the stairs. He loved it when she got like this.

I haveta fuck the little bitch, he'd say to himself. She wants it so bad I feel sorry for her.

At the top of the stairs they turned completely around and walked down the hallway. Leaks had eroded some parts of the ceiling, exposing patches of the next floor up.

"Is there an attic?" Debbie asked.

"There's nuthin' up there."

They poked their heads through doorways and saw more neglected rooms. One with tons of bottles and beer cans where people had partied, another with wood splintered all over its floor. Ray disappeared to a room and called to her.

Debbie found him lying on a mattress in the middle of a room that wasn't so trashed. There was a sheet and a grey electric blanket on it.

"Welcome to my parlor."

Debbie plopped down next to him. There was a window on the side to their right and another facing out toward the house's backyard. The ceiling had a shoebox-sized hole that peered through to the attic.

"I tole you to fix that leaky roof," she said.

Ray wasted no time, and his hands wandered all over her as if she were a hunk of clay to be sculpted. One was up her shirt clutching at her breast the way a child's hand moves inside a sock puppet. The other explored the gorge between her legs, pulsing at the crotch of blue jeans.

"Ray baby. I'm real horny," Debbie whispered between damp kisses.

He rolled over on top of her, dry humping as she parted her legs. Twilight gathered outside the windows and the room grew dim as heavy breaths and sighs filled it.

Soon they were down to their underwear and Ray's mouth lapped at her covered crotch.

Cotton candy, he thought. The crotch of her light pink panties was soaked so that he could see through to the tufts of dark pubic hair. Ray's fingers peeled back the cotton lips and found the brown patch silky as a soaked cat o'nine tail. Debbie moaned as he slipped his first two fingers into the noodly wetness.

"God, I love yer fingers," she whispered between gasps.

Ray rubbed himself against her leg to remind her that he needed some attention. Her hand reached down and stroked the taut shaft and his fingers made a trigger-pulling motion inside her, causing wet clicks to go off.

"I wish they could be inside me all the time," she gasped in his ear.

She tugged the panties down herself and Ray lowered his face into her. Debbie moved to meet his tongue and he wondered whether he'd betray himself and come. His neck strained as his mouth gobbled, and the tangy juice filmed his face as he sucked.

Debbie lay with her eyes closed and her fingers stroked through Ray's short hair. Sometimes she wished that she could just have his head for a pet; a head that couldn't talk, but could eat her out for hours. She felt his tongue wiggling and her body was slowly going up a mountain. Her longing trudged higher and his tongue kept licking and flicking and her fingers squeezed his hair until she was sailing off the mountain top, drifting down on a carpet of supreme satisfaction.

"Yer slicker'n snot on a doorknob."

She opened her eyes and let out an enormous breath as she stared at the hole in the ceiling above them. Debbie thought she saw a finger curving around the opening and she lifted Ray's head from between her legs.

"Ray honey, are you sure we're alone?"

"'Course."

"I think I just saw something movin' 'round that hole."

Ray glanced up as his fingers continued to slide into her.

"You was seein' things. It's gittin' dark."

Debbie closed her eyes again and spread her legs further as Ray's thumb drilled into the marsh of her opening.

"Ray baby. Don't stop."

His thrusts quickened and he watched her face straddle beams of pleasure. Debbie's eyes opened again to glance at Ray and then she focused her gaze upward. This time she saw an eye perched above the hole, staring down at her.

"Ray! Ray!"

Debbie pushed his hand away from her and sat up.

"Ray, there's someone up there. I saw someone lookin' at me."

She grabbed at the blanket and draped it over herself.

"Look!"

Ray looked up at the opening in the ceiling, but saw nothing except the empty space of the attic above.

"I don't see nuthin'."

"Ray, I swear. You gotta go see what's up there."

Ray ran his hand along her leg.

"Baby, I'm about to bust."

"Ray, there's someone up there! I'm not touchin' you 'til you go look."

He rolled off the mattress and silently sulked as he tugged his underwear and jeans back on. Ray slipped on his shoes without tying them and headed for the door.

"Don't go nowhere," he muttered.

Dusk was slowly pouring in from outside, giving everything a purplish-blue tinge. Ray spotted the faded horizon through the window.

Titty nipple pink, he thought.

He bounded up the back stairs and entered the room above theirs. There was nothing remarkable about it and Ray stuck his face through the hole in the floor to gaze at Debbie.

"Flash me some titty!" Ray hollered.

"What's up there?" Debbie asked.

"Just a horny toad with a big long tongue."

"I swear I saw somepin."

"No one's up 'ere."

"Come back. I'm gittin' lonely."

Ray glanced out the back window of the room at the old leaning barn in the distance. He decided to take one last look around and went to the closet door.

Did I just imagine seein' fingers while Ray's were inside me? Debbie wondered. Did I think I saw a face when Ray's was buried down there?

The smell of the sweaty soak drying between her legs disgusted Debbie. It made her feel grimy like the truck windshield constantly pelted with dirt and dead bugs, never able to get clean.

She thought about the blow job she'd have to give Ray, and how he wouldn't let her know when he was about to come so that the warm salty spew nearly gagged her. Maybe she could get away with a hand job, but they usually took so long that her arm nearly fell off.

Ray returned and peeled off his clothes in the gathering twilight.

"I guess I was seein' things. Baby, I missed you," Debbie cooed.

Ray crawled under the electric blanket and eased Debbie over onto her stomach.

"What're you doin'?"

His hands began to massage her bare ass and Debbie closed her eyes to concentrate on the sensation. The squeezing relaxed her and she eased her legs farther apart. Ray took this cue to let his fingers wander between them and into the welcoming crevice. Debbie heaved a great breath as she humped like a slow wave against the shore of his probing fingers. She lifted herself up to meet him and his other hand crept underneath her so that more fingers could enter her.

"Baby, you've ne'er done me like this," she said between pants. "Yer fingers..."

Debbie broke off and shuddered with delight as his thrusts drew to a feverish speed in the darkness. A tide of raw energy swept through her and she moved mindlessly like a mad machine powered by pleasure.

Suddenly, Ray stopped. Debbie moved greedily.

"More, baby. God don't stop," her husky drawl bruised.

Ray's soaking fingers circled around her asshole, and she felt a tickling sensation. She felt like she was perched atop an Easter outhouse with a draft coming from below. Then he inserted the end of his finger into her and she drew back.

His hand gripped at one of the cheeks of her ass and it felt like her backside was a flag in the breeze. Debbie felt his fingers there again, brushing slightly at the tight opening, and she ground her face into the mattress and reached her own hand around to grab at the other side of her ass.

His finger slowly inched into her and she pulled herself open wider. The pain went straight to her head and tears welled in her eyes, but there was something exciting about feeling him there.

Soon, he inserted his whole finger and she reached her other hand around so that she spread both her ass cheeks. It felt good and bad and dirty and beautiful all at once. She couldn't move herself, but the finger slowly prodded into the tiny hole, creating eddies and whirlpools of pleasure.

She felt another finger buzzing around the opening like a bee near a flower. Debbie shivered as the finger skittered around her asshole. She pried herself open as wide as she could and felt both fingers dart in like tiny minnows. Debbie never knew she could be so wet there, and her thumbs ached from wedging herself open.

Her orgasm came quick and furious, draining her of energy, and she collapsed in exhaustion. Debbie lay on her stomach panting, trying to gather the pieces of herself that seemed to be dangled and strewn every which way.

Debbie felt down there. Then she felt Ray's breath between her legs again, and he slowly rolled her over and kissed the insides of her thighs.

"Is it as soft as eyelids down there?" she asked. But Ray's mouth was too busy to respond.

"Baby, enough already."

Debbie felt something slip out of her and she reached down between her legs. Her fingers pawed at the mattress, and she reached inside herself and touched something strange. She pulled it out, and turned it over in her hand. Her other hand dragged out another one, and a hollow fear gripped her as she realized she was holding two fingers.

Debbie's eyes strained in the darkness to see the thing staring down at her through the hole in the ceiling. It was perfectly still and perfectly dreadful, and gleamed in the darkness.

She reached down at the head between her legs and felt the mask of skin from its face peel off.

"Ray?"

But she knew it wasn't Ray.

Ray was up there. Lifeless. Staring. Faceless.

Debbie's heart surged in her chest like a clapper propelled by a carnival strongman's sledge. A strange face leered at her and smiled when she launched into her first scream.

RESTORATION

Heather Corinna

It was like one on a cherub in the corners of a Tintoretto. That's how perfect it was. I noticed her mouth before I could see anything else. I'd even been retouching one as she came in, the tip of my brush covered in an alizarine so pink it'd make an old woman blush. Alizarine crimson: the pinks of the Venus' thighs, of the rosy nipples on Lucretia, on the blood on the hands of every Jesus, sometimes tempered with a bit of a carmine, sometimes dimmed down with sepias to keep the Puritans from turning away in shame.

There was alizarine on my brush, and there was that mouth.

"I'm looking for Elisabetta O'Donnell."

Dear God, that mouth. My hands were covered in paint, covered in that amazing hue, and I wiped them on the thighs of my jeans, trying to pull my eyes from those cherubic lips.

"Liza," I said, trying to tone down the flustered smile I felt terrorizing my face.

She'd put out her hand shyly. "Good to meet you. Do you know where I can find her?"

"I'm sorry," I just laughed, nervously. The soft plump of that mouth had me beside myself. "I'm Elisabetta. Call me Liza."

She laughed then, too, a high chirp like the perfect song of a bird at dawn, and a soft blush, more a carmine than a crimson, spread over her cheeks.

"Oh, it's good to meet you. I said that already." She walked up to the old crackling piece I was retouching and tilted her head, studying it. "That painting looks very old."

A voice like soft honey.

"1670, as best as I can tell. A portrait from the Tzar of Russias' estate. They found it just last week. It's in pretty bad shape. The technique the artist used involved a lot of thin layers, you can see how they flake here, and the paint seems like it was thinned out a lot to begin with. Doesn't make for permanence." I laughed at myself. I've been working too much. "I'm sorry, you're probably not interested. What can I do for you, Ms…?"

"How sad, when you think that perhaps permanence is what we most strive for."

She put out her hand again, squeezing mine when I took it. Her palms were a little damp, and with that mouth in my eyes and the moist sweat seeping into my palms, a shiver crawled over my arm.

"No 'Ms.', please. Madeline Taylor. Madeline is fine."

I squeezed the hand, studying the fragile thin bones under her alabaster skin. I had to shake my head, break my reverie. "Madeline. What can I do for you?"

"Professor Poncet from the University highly recommended you." I couldn't help but laugh. I couldn't help but wonder what exactly it was Sarah Poncet was recommending me for. God knows she certainly wouldn't recommend me for much after the way we'd broken up.

"For…?" I could hear the incredulousness in my voice. I really have to cut that out, stop being so transparent.

She smiled a little bit. Maybe Sarah didn't have the hard feelings I'd thought she had. Dear God, look at that mouth.

"I have something I'd like to have restored. It's very dear to me. It's—very important it be fully restored, if it can."

Her eyes looked distant for a minute there. "Do you have it with you?"

She shook her head. "No, I'm afraid not. I prefer not to take it out of my home. As I said, it has a very intimate value to me."

I saw my hands as I waved them, covered in paint. What a mess. "That's not a problem," I heard myself say. "Would you like me to come look at it? I actually have some time now." No, I don't. What am I saying? I have a class in an hour. Too late to take it back now.

She smiled. I quivered; I could feel something loosen under the old denim. "Really? I don't live far from here, I could drive us over. I'd—of course—pay you for your time, even if you don't decide to do the restoration."

I tossed my smock onto the stool and slid the plastic over my palette, before I caught a blush on her cheeks again. Shit. I almost laughed, but I just redid the top three buttons on my shirt that sat undone, exposing my hard nipple to those eyes, to that mouth. That shiver, again.

I fought to gain ground with this poised bird. "I get really involved when I'm working. Good thing for the smock." Real witty there, Liza.

She laughed—*oh thank you*—buttoning her coat. She gestured to the door as I slid my velvet jacket over my arms. Her tongue flicked out over her lips for a minute, wetting them as I followed her out.

Dear God, that mouth.

It was an unbelievable piece. Under all the flaking layers, the lines, the light, the shading were remarkable, and the lips on the ivory face were like rose petals, like hers.

I couldn't help but notice the likeness. She'd said she noticed it herself, it had been in her family for years, it was priceless. She'd wanted me to start working on it immediately, had no trouble dealing with my fee, and I had no trouble agreeing immediately even though I had a thousand other assignments I was completely behind on, and knew I should have said no, and that I was going to have a lot of explaining to do at the museum.

She wanted it done awfully fast. It was a wreck, this piece.

Normally it'd have taken me weeks, even months to do something like this, and I'd said as much. Then she'd started to cry, that rosebud mouth trembling as she bit into it.

"I have to have it, now, " she'd said. "I am not sure how to make you understand how dire it is."

Her fingers had traced over the edges of the lips on the canvas. Something was tugging at me, something that didn't feel like the shiver I was getting from her lips, more like a shiver when someone touches you the wrong way, or when the air is too cold to be comfortable, and you can't pretend a nice draft is refreshing. Breezes are one thing. Icy winds are just cold.

But I couldn't say no. Not to those trembling lips.

"I brought you some coffee."

Hooker's green, vermillion, just some of the ultramarine right there. Almost.

"Liza?" That voice. Like a bell.

I set the brush in my teeth and rubbed my eyes. It was late. The moon shone over her hair, playing a blue sheen over the light gold. She looked rumpled and her eyes looked bleary. Her lips were wet.

I reached over and spun down the volume on the box, and the sounds of the cello whispered instead of shouted. I turned around on the stool and took the cup. She was in a black silk robe.

No such thing as black that is only black, even the mars black shines with something else. Sometimes it has bits of blue in it, sometimes, green. There was crimson in this one, on the faint shine of it in the half-light.

"I woke you. I'm sorry."

She shook her head, studying the painting. "I don't sleep well, I've been restless forever. You've almost finished."

I looked at it again, wiping my hands on my sweaty torso underneath the old silk camisole. "I'm close."

She leaned over my shoulder. I felt her hair tickle my bare skin, like feathers. My chest rippled with goosebumps, and I could see my nipples raised through the antique silk, endless betrayers of the cool facade I tried to wear over my libido.

"The mouth… It's so perfect." Her lips were at my ear, and her breath was warm. I heard myself gasp, and swallowed, feeling my fingers shake.

"It was a perfect mouth to begin with. It drew me in." My hands had a life of their own and dared to tangle themselves in a stray curl of her hair as it looped over my chest.

"I was drawn in myself," she whispered.

She kissed my ear as she whispered that. That mouth drew me in.

I turned on the stool and ran my fingers over it, along the soft heart inside, where it was wet and red and open.

I had to have it, everywhere. I covered it with mine in a hungry rush, overturning the stool.

Alizarine crimson, napthol red, alabaster.

That mouth: on the burnt sienna of my nipple, on the soft gold of my stomach, inside the pale yellow of my thighs, under the thick hansa yellow hair that draped across my legs, and between the fragile hands that worked inside my skin, over the slow tongue drawing out the shuddering and the shivers, drinking in the slick of my pleasure as the salt of her tears stung the open pinked flesh there, quaking under her lips.

That mouth, as it whispered into my ear as my fingers pulled and pressed it, as her muscles shook and her breath broke, as it cried gently amidst the sweat, the turpentine and the tarp, spotted prism violet, prussian blue, mars black.

"Finish the painting, please. Please."

That mouth, as it moved beneath me, her hands gripping the stool, her teeth nibbling on my wet thighs as I painted, the brush drizzling reds and golds and greens unto the canvas of her hair as I set on the last layer.

Those lips, as they brought me beyond any threshold of pleasure or pain I'd known, as they cried out when I set the last stroke to the worn fabric and I faded into the warmest, wettest oblivion I'd ever imagined, chaining me to their kiss forever.

Dear God, that mouth.

When I woke, I knew she was gone. I would have known anyway, simply because the scent of her wasn't beside me, and I laid alone on the tarp, covered in paint. I might have known if only because the salt of her sweat wasn't lingering on my skin, the scent, the taste of her wasn't on my fingers. When I called out for her, I knew it was out of habit more than much else; I knew before then she was gone, and she wasn't out bringing back breakfast, either.

Alizarine crimson: in flakes on my fingers, on my thighs, stuck in my teeth, falling from the canvas on the wall that was in horrible condition.

From that mouth.

It drew me in.

I mix the palette again, as I have so many times before. Alabaster, phthalocyanine green, cyan blue, vermillion, carmine yellow, light cobalt, napthol red, mars black.

And of course, alizarine crimson, wet as a cherub's mouth on a Tintoretto, in the pinks of the Venus' thighs, of the rosy nipples on Lucretia, on the blood on the hands of every Jesus, and on that mouth.

I touch the tip of my brush into the thick daub of paint, feeling my thighs loosen, a hot breath on my ear, a wet tongue on my skin as I begin to retouch the faded perfect bow of those lips.

Permanence is perhaps what we most strive for.

There is alizarine on my brush, and there is that mouth.

Dear God, that mouth.

BLUE

Jerry Juarez

They fucked and fucked. After their final argument forever, they fucked. He was tired of her success, beyond jealous, he never got to see her. And when she was home, she never left the telephone's side.

She really did care, she simply couldn't show it anymore. So much so that her pride had all been stepped on by him. She didn't understand his no motivation. His passions: hallucinogens, music, fuckety-fucking sex. How could a dick have kept them together for so long?

How could he compete against a hair studio, queer stylists and over-sexed clients? He was so blue-irate that his wife's passion turned from him towards her business. He'll get her back, he thought. He *was* known for his pony rides after all. Still, if it wasn't for work and for queers, she'd be home now. No galavanting to butt pirate clubs and for what?

He would hurt himself to make her stay. So many threats

of suicide… but she knew he wasn't crying wolf. She loved him that much. How could she leave? In another man's arms? No way! The next best thing: a gay guy. Still, she did need to fuck and without some hovering cloud of blue despair called love. The next best thing: pussy (women).

Being normal (functional) wasn't easy… Prozac, Paxil, St. John's Wort. Born blue, live blue, die blue. Had already done lost time, yes, finally he'd show her, "This is what you're going to miss *mamita*!" As his gaze turned towards the backyard, his eye caught that great oak tree. "You'll see," he says.

Too much symbolism can lead to tunnel vision. When she doesn't check herself, she dwells on that branch. How he hated those queers but how she needed them, especially now. With her strength diminished, her impatience omnipotent, and the sting of her banged come-filled cunt he gave her last night, she cut off that tree branch all by herself. "Dead and dangling," she says, is how he was found. So why was she still thinking of his sex?

TWO SIDES TO EVERY STORY

Dani Bauter

> *"I wish I could be stranded*
> *inside your body*
> *become one of the impulses*
> *that flicker across your synapses*
> *become one of your urges"*
> *—Debra Boxer*

HANNAH

I went to a fortune teller once. And she told me that I would soon recognize all of the beautiful people around me. I would see the potential in everyone and everything, and as a result I would find my true love. And she was right. Ofelia was a friend of my co-worker, and she walked into my life but then walked right back out. This is my account of what happened, right down to the very last moment. Everything in this account is true, I swear on it.

I honestly believed we were perfect for each other, but at first Ofelia didn't see it. She begged me to stop loving her because the intensity of my love scared her. I argued that it was only because I was suffering from my passion for her—and what is sex and love without passion? (Emphasis on the sex part.) Eventually she let herself be open to me, and my insatiable desires. The sex blew both of our minds, it was really that good.

Ofelia had a body that would not quit—or even take a break, for that matter. I guess I let my clit be the mistress of my every decision when it came to Ofelia. I never realized that I was really just pushing her away when I acted like that—I don't really understand it now even. I thought I could explain all of my desires to her in writing—that being a writer and editor herself she would understand. I have a tendency to overdo things sometimes though.

But I remember the first time we met; it was the first time that a woman in her league had ever given me the time of day. She had come into my work to talk to Jesse, and I saw him point her in my direction. *What's up with that?* I wondered, but before I had a chance to think further about it she was standing in front of me.

Ofelia was wearing a little sundress that showed off her long tanned legs and platform sandals. Her curly hair was down and covered half of her back, I watched her tuck a piece behind her ear and smile shyly. "I'm a friend of Jesse's. He told me you could hook me up with some paint if I ask sweetly. Would you do me a favor?"

This honey's eyes were light brown, almost yellow, and they were putting me in a trance. I pulled away from her for a second and reminded myself that I am a stud who's gonna score big time tonight. "Trade you a favor for a favor. You give me your number, I give you the paint. What do you think?"

Ofelia smiled and reached for my hand. She turned it over and grabbed a nearby pen. She started writing the digits on the inside, then wrote her name underneath. I licked my lips and looked down at her curls, already thinking about what I could use to harness them all back when it was time to do some serious fucking. When she was done I fulfilled my promise and gave her the paint. She gave me a long and suggestive look, then asked when she should expect my call. I smirked and shrugged my shoulders. "Soon," I replied.

I called her that night, of course. Who could leave a hotty like that hanging? I set up a time to pick her up the next evening to go watch a movie. I didn't plan to ever leave her house, though. I wanted to ravage her so bad because I felt like it had been too long since I had seen her.

As soon as she opened the door I started kissing her really deeply, and got us onto the bed pretty quickly. She was moaning quietly, which told me that I was doing something right. I wanted to taste her though, I wanted to run my tongue all up under her clit and then use my finger to find her g-spot. I wanted to taste some creamy girl-semen, the ejaculate I was sure that a woman like Ofelia could shoot. Even my most elaborate fantasies had never played out this spicy. I would have remembered that.

So nice and full of laughter, so beautiful and intelligent. If only I weren't married and raising my three-year-old daughter. If circumstances were different, I would make her mine and arrange it so she wouldn't have to work and she could write her stories all day long.

Dear Ofelia,

I was thinking of you all day, I hope I get to see you tomorrow. I miss you. I know the time we spend together isn't much but I replay everything in my mind over and over again. There's parts in my life that make me not want to live, but you cheer me up.

Ofelia, I only wish I could have one full day with you alone. I bet I could make you come so hard you'd feel tingles all over your body for about a week. We still haven't used your handcuffs yet, soon hopefully. I can't help but think of your breasts in my mouth and my lips and tongue yearning to slowly caress your clit. I love the smell and the taste of your pussy. I crave it all day nonstop, I'm hungry now, can you feed me tomorrow?

Love,

Hannah

Ofelia didn't really take too kindly to this note I sent her. I thought it was pretty nice. But I guess we have different taste, which is OK. One of the sacrifices I'd be willing to make to be with her.

It took me a while before I could tell Ofelia the truth about me, that I am married and have a daughter. I was afraid she would judge me, and not want anything to do with me because I am not what she thought. Yeah, I know, typical Sally Jesse bullshit.

I didn't really get the choice though when I got a call from my husband while she was visiting me at work, and it was an emergency—my little daughter had fallen and hurt her head. She's fine now, though. I decided then just to bite the bullet and tell her. And she was a little surprised, but never one to judge or shock easily, she went with it. I was so relieved, and now it felt like I could really be myself with her, even more than before. I told her that she should come by my house to meet my daughter, and she enthusiastically agreed. I couldn't believe my good fortune.

And she did actually come by my house, one Wednesday after I got off work she picked me up and took me home. We played with my daughter for a little while and then we decided to chill and watch some TV. We ended up all over each other on the couch, I guess I just couldn't keep my paws off of her. I had to taste her again though, and she was on the rag. I didn't care, I put my face between her legs and licked her clean.

Right when we had finished up and I held her during her last orgasm, there was a knock at the door. My cousin. Who said he'd been watching through the peephole and couldn't believe what he'd just seen. It was then that I really thought about what I was doing and how I was gonna get into some serious trouble if I kept this up. I couldn't help it though. Ofelia was just too fine and sweet and I was whipped. I wondered if she knew how much she was saving me just by hanging around.

Dear Ofelia,

You look really pretty with your hair up. I'm glad you came to the hardware store today. I know we just met but I think about you a lot, and I miss you. I wish I didn't have so many responsibilities, so I could be with you. I don't know if you feel the same way but I find you attractive and I find myself daydreaming about you.

Ofelia, the last thing I want to do is hurt you, but since I'm married I'm kind of trapped for now. I guess I'm searching for a soulmate. Someone who I can share everything with: emotions, thoughts, and affections. I'm hoping that with time you and I can be together.

Kisses,

Hannah

I decided after a few weeks with Ofelia that I had to stop getting high with her because there was no telling what I would do, most of the time I would end up doing something embarrassing because I was all over her no matter who was around. I couldn't help it, and the bud just brought it out even more. She would still get stoned, though. I liked it because she became more of a freak, and it seemed the herb intensified all of the sensations around her erogenous zones. I loved to fuck her with my dildo, or wake her up by sucking her nipples first lightly then harder, and then biting them quickly, watching her eyes open in alarm but smiling when I looked at her with concern.

I loved the way she would transform her room into an erotic lair complete with lava lamp and incense, and the smell of just-smoked marijuana would come wafting out of the room when I opened the door. She would greet me with a smirk and nothing underneath that purple velour robe she always wore, and I would look at my watch, noting what time I had to be back from my lunch break.

I think I forgot to mention that I was Ofelia's first, her first taste of pussy that is. When I think about it now I guess she was having a hard time of it, coming out to others is difficult but coming out to yourself is even harder. Her dad didn't like it at all—but it wasn't only the gay part about her he couldn't stand, it was her choice of a lover. He hated me. I still to this day don't know why.

Ofelia stopped responding to my expressions of love for her—teddy bears, flowers, love notes. I don't think it was all her dad's influence. There was something inside her that was withdrawing from everyone, not just me. But it hurt me so bad that she didn't want to see me so much anymore that I had to see her, and tell her what she was making me contemplate.

It was the last time I saw her alive. She didn't look very happy. She had lost weight and her skin had a translucent color. This wasn't the woman I had fallen in love with. She stayed with me for a couple of minutes then told me she had to go, without so much as a kiss goodbye. The next day I got a phone call from Jesse—Ofelia had gone to the lake and drowned herself. He was barely conscious as he relayed the story; he had been up the whole night answering the pigs' questions and he needed to sleep. So I hung up the phone and raced over there, a million thoughts running through my mind and my body in auto-pilot.

Ofelia looked so peaceful and beautiful, more beautiful than I ever could have imagined. Her eyes were wide open and I saw in them what had made me love her in the first place. Her passion, her clarity, her warmth. It all came raging back at me as I stood there in her house and saw freedom. Independence. But not before letting her father know what I thought of him. In the past he had never hesitated to tell me exactly how much he hated the fact that his daughter was sleeping with me. Now it was my turn. And I planned to make it real good.

I set up a time for us to meet, telling him that I had something of Ofelia's that I thought he should have, "something very private," I said, making it sound really suggestive because I knew that would get to him. We met at the neighborhood bar and I bought him a beer, slipping a mickey in there when his head was turned. At least, I thought it was a mickey. Of course my dealer got my simple request mixed up and I really gave him something extraordinarily stronger. He never woke up, and rather than stay around and explain I fled from that bar as fast as my feet could carry me.

Now I didn't end up going that far. I'm just around the corner at the local motel. I got my own dose of freedom right here in my hand. "Ofelia, my darling, I will join you in a minute. 'Though this be madness, yet there is method in't.' "*

OFELIA

Have you ever had the feeling when someone is looking at you that they are devouring you, that they are eating every inch of your flesh just by taking you in with their eyes? That is what Hannah made me feel like from the first moment I

* Excerpt from *Hamlet*, Act II, scene 2, William Shakespeare

met her. Jesse sent me over to her department when I had to go into his work to buy paint for our house. She tried to act all butch when I asked her for a favor, she even tried to get my number. So I gave it to her, I don't know why. Some people have a kind of sex appeal that seems to come from nowhere, yet they can project it like nobody's business. That was Hannah. I was hoping she would call me and she didn't let me down; it's not like I mac on girls all of the time it's cause she made me wonder what it would actually be like. She looked kinda sexy in her Levi's and Goodman's Hardware T-shirt and I thought why not?

I was feeling pretty good about myself when I saw her for the first time outside of work. She met me at my house where I lived with a couple of my friends, and we managed to spend the sixty minutes allotted for her lunch break in very compromising positions. She could make me so hot just by kissing me, and the way she licked my pussy was addicting. I loved to get high and wait for her to come to me, wearing only my robe and my finest-smelling lotion, soaking the bedspread with my juices already flowing down my legs. It was her keys that always got to me though. The way she wore them on a chain on her belt and never took them off, using their coldness to bring my nipples to attention or tickle my clit while she went down on me.

I was drawn to her and repelled by her at the same time. She could give me the best sex I'd ever experienced but her flattery and gestures of love both surprised and frightened me. I would often open our front door to teddy bears with "I Love You" emblazoned across their tummies or a single red rose with a note attached that announced how much she wanted me.

Besides that though was the little problem about my family. My dad never liked her, it's like he instinctively knew that hanging around her would be trouble. And now that we can talk again he has confirmed it. He never trusted Hannah, he thought that her madness would drive everyone around her crazy. He told me that with people like her it starts out really subtle, and then builds up into an explosion of insanity. A lot of good that does me, knowing that now. One good thing is that Hannah is not around. She never made it up here. What dreams may come led her to another destiny.

My family shunned me when I came out to them. My dad made clear his intentions of never speaking to me until I became straight again. My sisters wouldn't have anything to do with me. The only people I really had in my life were my two best friends, Jesse and his boyfriend Tito. I really tried to stay strong. I didn't know where to go, though. I continued to see Hannah but I knew I wasn't gaining anything by doing so. When she told me about her husband and daughter I was a little thrown off guard but her sex kept beckoning me so I never stopped seeing her. I knew I was just adding fuel to the fire of family problems but I didn't know where else to go.

I find sanctuary in floating nowadays. Floating in the lake where my uncertainties and unspoken fears lie. Sometimes I wanted to run from all of the pain, but it was a pain borne of my own insecurities and feelings of insufficiency. I wanted to please everyone and somehow please myself. I wondered why

I felt crippled by emotions so strong I would curl into a ball and try to will them away. They wouldn't go. Neither would my heartache, my loneliness, and my awareness of others' hardships. Eventually these screams melted into one dull ache of unhappiness. I longed to escape, but I feared my unhappiness would shadow me.

Trust was the emotion I lacked so thoroughly. I could never love another as my own. Unbeknownst to those I took to my bed, my heart was always vulnerably open and exposed like a battle wound. This was beyond my control. I feared the iron wrist of my father, who turned my whole family against me in a fit of anger. I could only wait for the love I so desperately desired to transform me.

Before all of the pain emerged I was a naive and happy child. I remember that, it wasn't that long ago. Although I could never escape my lingering insecurity and shyness, I could enjoy life that much more readily. I didn't always feel like I was waiting. Waiting to inhale the smog-and worry-free lifestyle that had graced me at childbirth. When drugs pervaded my own private atmosphere, I welcomed them with open arms. I pushed the worries and warnings to the back of my feeble mind and focused on the too temporary respite from reality.

Drugs became my new lovers, and my life turned into a syndicated series of waiting to inhale. I had a new remedy. It really wasn't so bad through my stony haze. But through the illusion of reality I was still hurting badly. And when I ran out of drugs and had to face my family I had nowhere to go again.

I had shunned Hannah long before and that night when she decided to stop by for a visit I could barely stand spending five minutes with her. I walked right off that porch to the lake, shedding my clothes as I drew closer. I kept walking until I couldn't float anymore, until I was submerged in water and I finally felt at home. I had somewhere to go. I finally had somewhere to go.

NOW

Cecilia Tan

Now I'm putting my hands onto Sander's shoulders, slick hot with sweat, one knee sliding past his thigh as I climb onto the bench. Now I'm trying not to look into his eyes because I don't know if we'll end up together. I can feel the tip of his cock on my inner thigh as I wait for the bell to ring. Now is the moment I have waited for all day, when this shy newcomer would be naked under me. Now I shudder in anticipation.

Twenty minutes ago we were flying, engines running hot in the fog-thick atmosphere, each of us plugged in tight to our machines, from hands to brains, fingertips flicking us through the sky, as fast as thought. I could feel the water smoke edges of clouds shredding against my arms/my wings. I knew I was not really touching the methane-heavy air, but the sensors work.

I was plugged in and not separate from my machine. It was as if I dove through the sky, as if I skimmed the surface of the sea, even though I never left the Tank.

Two minutes from now I'll be on Cirzon's lap, his impressive cock lodged in me. I'll be clinging to his neck, pressing my ear to his close-cropped hair, sweat running down our backs as I try to sink all the way down. I'll wish he could reach up and fit his hands over my hips, pull me down snug onto him, but in this game, he cannot help. Two minutes from now, he will sit like all the other men, rigid on the bench, because those are the rules. The women circle until the bell rings, and then we climb on.

But now. Now I am poised above Sander. He came to the squad only two weeks ago, and some of the others do not know him or trust him, yet. But I have been watching him, wondering, seeing his eyes in my dreams and wanting to approach him. I can almost feel Nulia's gaze on me, next to me on Bhujan's lap, watching to see what I'll do, now that he is between my legs. I do nothing but wait for the bell, my thighs trembling, resting my lips on the top of his dark head.

Two hours ago our ships were out on reconnaissance, skimming the surface dotted with wrecked buildings, looking for the enemy, and not finding him. Or her. The squad of thirteen divided, nine below, four above, but nothing to see but toppled trees and the broken teeth of the punched out skyline.

Two hours from now I'll be in Cirzon's quarters, my hands braced against the edges of the bunk, while his tongue roots around between my legs, like a slinth hungry for sweet fruit pulp. But I won't be able to tell him of my hunger, of the reason I left decompression unsatisfied. He'll think he knows why, and I'll let him, as I let him eat me. Two hours from now, he'll spell his name with his tongue between my lips, as he hooks two thumbs inside me, bony firm and preparing me to take all of him in.

Thirty seconds ago, we were circling the bench, the men sitting in two rows back to back, each of us wondering who would be matched with whom. With each synchronized step, I came to another man in my squad until the one empty place was before me. But then I came to Alden, and Nulia stood before the empty place. Seven of us, six of them. Who would be the odd woman out? We continued to circle, and as I came to Sander, my wish came true and the bell rang.

Three minutes from now I'll still be clinging to Cirzon on the bench, my cunt too tight in this position to really take him in, frantically rubbing my clit on his smooth sweat slick stomach. Cirzon has almost no hair on his body and I will curse this fact, silently, as I struggle and fail to find any friction against him. I won't want to come with him, I'll be wishing that the random bell had rung in my favor and left me with Sander. But I will want to come, will want to bring both of us to climax, because then we will be out of the game and there will be no chance for me to be the odd woman out. I can hunt Sander at my leisure later, shy boy only frightened by my hunger. Three minutes from now I will be trying to come, rubbing my hard nipples over the sculpted smooth chest of Cirzon, and failing.

One hour ago, I heard Sander's voice in my ear: "This one's almost intact."

We wheeled in the sky, our ships realigning themselves to

his location, and we came to a low group of buildings, a school maybe, next to a lake. But even the closest buzz provoked no sign of our quarry.

Now the bell rings and I sink onto Sander's cock, barely catching the sound in my throat before it escapes. No cries or moans are allowed in the game of Bell Bell—silence is the rule. I swallow my grateful sigh and let my thighs piston me up and down. Sander is slight and shivering beneath me, as badly in need of release as I am, and I am trying to get us there. We fit together well—surely he feels it too, I think. In my mind I already see us in my quarters, taking our time with each other, licking and talking and him betwen my legs for hours. I want him to want me. I am going as fast as I can, squeezing my cunt tight, hoping to take us both out of the game.

One minute from now, I'll bite my lip in frustration, as the bell rings and I must move on.

Two hours and fifteen minutes from now I'll be clawing Cirzon's back while he does what he does best besides fly. He'll be making me scream, and I'll have forgotten that there are boundaries to my body, that it is not me that cuts through the clouds, that it is not me that grunts and shudders with the strain. Plugged in and not separate.

Ten minutes ago we emerged from the Tank, blinking visions of alien skies from our eyes. The game of Bell Bell began and I watched Nulia climb on Cirzon with delight.

Ten minutes from now the game will end with me in the empty space and Nulia and Sander the only two left not spent. I will stand at attention while she licks salt sweat from his face, while she rocks her hips and drags her clit over the thin ridge of dark fur that sprouts from his crotch and tendrils up to his belly button. I will watch her head fall back and the flush spread over her skin as she comes.

A hundred years ago, a squad commander invented Bell Bell, to provide a disciplined structure for the release of the sexual arousal that full body flying inevitably created. For what is a Kylar without discipline? We emerge from the Tank soaked in neuro-stimulants, our skins humming with tension and lust, just as her crew had. She knew, too, that tradition and tactics would always leave her an odd woman out. But that is the discipline of the squad, of the battle. When not on alert, her crew squandered precious sleep hours to penetrate each other more recreationally. Or for love.

Two hours from now I'll be playing my own game of Bell Bell with Cirzon, as he fills me past aching and tires me out. I'll be swallowing the name my mouth wants to cry, Silence is the rule. But that will be then. Now, Sander is in my arms, and now Sander is in my cunt, and now Sander is in my heart, and I don't want to let go.

THE EUCHARIST

Jarboe

At barely twenty, the girl can now remember little about herself before she came here to the convent. Before the addiction began. Before you, Sister—her pusher.

Her body is flushed from the scalding Japanese-style baths but the imprints of your fingers and the stain of your saliva remains indelible. Playful nibbles have scarred her flesh. Fresh scabs have begun to form on her bruised and welted breasts in a useless attempt to heal where they will be reopened in your eager feeding. You lift her breasts up to your mouth as a priest raises the chalice. The dark purple is dramatic against her white skin. She is your food and she's writhing in your name.

Salvation is found within these stone walls.

Didn't you yourself promise her such awareness that nothing could be as it was before? All of the girl's former personalities will die soon as you continue to inject a persuasive and nebulous belief. You keep her in an endorphin zone. She trembles under your tongue lavishing yet another orgasm, in the process of self deterioration towards becoming the craving.

Look how swollen is our lovely daughter, anoint these in the oil flavored with anise. Ahhhhh... there. She smiles even as she sleeps. Let's give her a goodnight kiss on both pairs of those glistening lips.

And she is smiling because she is numb. She doesn't bother to count her orgasms any more. She knows you will stop soon, Sister. And she can rest for a few hours until this 'administering' begins again. Salacity has become simultaneous torment. And she's a caged bird who stays inside when the door is swung open.

Later, she wakes from her dream state to the continuing dream inside this room. In the shadows are the sounds of the walls breathing and motion and leather in the dark corner. A silhouette emerges into the moonlight; boyish hair but distinctly feminine form interrupted by the dildo strapped in all its ribbed and shiny glory onto curving hips.

Sister, your face is calm and sublime as you step towards the bed and sigh ever so subtly in anticipation. You used to do penance for what you first perceived as your gluttony, the absurd persistent hunger—but of course, that has changed through she who waits quietly and opens her legs wide in reverence. She is to turn over at the mere glance of instruction. Her mouth is moist and open. She is ready to receive you. And all you can do now is admire her humility. She is grace.

Your virgin martyr.

You are very skilled with your dildo as beneath the girl you penetrate and together you throb. She is raw inside from your nightly visits. As the girl straddles you, you suckle while stabbing hard up into her, a plunging syringe of burning Eucharist. Her breasts are so chafed and tender that she winces even as she swoons in beatitude when like the Lilith you are, your teeth rip down into her without mercy in your own now anxious need.

The girl is fully compliant in the agony and obediently continues the offering of her swollen blue and red breasts in her divine servitude over your face, Sister—the face of the perverted celibate—as you eat of her body. You move in sync between the unstoppable rushes of the communion of your mutual orgiastic fix. Smearing the girl's buttocks with blood, you fiercely deliver her while deep in her rectum as she screams and you masturbate in a blinding frenzy for the glory of God.

Enraptured, you are both pure in prayer and do not question as you worship—that you are indeed Found.

IN HER WAKE

Amy Rasmussen

When she spilled into my hands she was finally and forever mine, but I had lost her already.

The friends who came to console me were lost as well, for what to say or do. Only I walked among them without fear or hesitation. For once I knew just what to do. You see, she spoke to me still, her breath against mine.

I began with, “I need this,” very roughly.

The first fellow delivers flowers, a stranger.

I step out onto the sidewalk wearing just her panties, my tits flagging passerby. He shoves me inside and, the door still open, I force his wet mouth to my nipple. “Suck!” I yell, and he does. “Bite,” I demand, I scream. He wrenches away from me. Dark clumps of his hair fall from my hands to the floor. He opens his pants and his buoyant hard-on points at me. He merely grasps the tip and his cock gushes forth, splashing my feet. He shivers and is gone, the shutting door spreading his seed across the floor.

A knock.

My underwear in my hands, I soak up the come, smear the floorboards, then pull the panties back on. I am naked but for the wet tug at my crotch, his juice still hot against me. I pull open the door.

My neighbor, the pastor, is wide eyed, sees my grief, steps inside. I shut the door and wrestle him to the floor. He does not struggle. "I've got something inside me," I cry, rolling into a ball. "You've got to take it out!" His hands press against my upper arms, pinning me. "It's killing me, the pain!" I'm crying, then I push ineffectively at my soiled panties, demanding, "Take them off."

He pauses.

"It hurts!"

I'm too loud now; he complies, pulls at them with one hand, off one hip first, then the next, works them down to my knees. "Reach in and pull it out." I say. I pull his hand between my legs, insistent. He resists, then looks me in the eye.

He slips a ginger finger into my slit, leaning over so he doesn't have to look at me.

"It's killing me!" I wail. I pull at his wrist, and his thick fingers enter me, stretching me.

"Reach in all the way," I say, biting down on his ear, and as he forces his great hand past my pelvis I cry out, feeling the bones separate. My arms wrap around his neck as I hump his hand, hard. My forehead slams into his teeth. His coat cuff slaps my swollen lips, my tender clit.

Doorbell rings. I jump to and push him into the bathroom. It is his eldest son, holding a baking dish wrapped in tinfoil. "My mom..." he starts, almost dropping the dish. "Help me," I say, and as he steps across the threshold I know he has never been this close to a naked woman. He bends over to set the dish on a chair, and a string of saliva leaves his open mouth.

"Close the door." I say, then I pull his shirt up over his head. His arms linger in the air for a moment, and I dive at his crotch, claw at his pants.

He is stunned as I release his cock, purple and bulging. "On the floor." I demand, and he lies on his back, the cock hovering above his taut belly. I lower myself down on him, my sex sweating as it devours him. I rut against him madly, and he is as a small boat in rough water, then begins to thrust, too, and our hip bones slap and clash. My wetness keeps the great mass between his legs, swells, won't let him escape. I pulse about him, my pussy a beating heart, squeezing the blood from his great vein. His hot emission washes into me and I immediately retreat, lie down on the floor, push his body away.

"Get your father," I say.

"What?" he says, then, "Dad, what are you—"

"I'm pregnant." I wail. "Hold hands! Both of you."

They gape at me. But I need them; they are part of the magic. They have to know. So I explain, "Before she died I thought I could never have her child. I thought I never could. But she's told me what to do."

The boys penis is finally flagging, his hand clasped to his father's, still wet and warm with me.

"I had to do it before she was buried. This seed in me is her and this child will be hers and mine. You both must say so!"

"We do," the pastor nods, and his son follows suit.

BRANDED

Rebecca Kissel

I'm terrified. And the funny thing is, I'm terrified by something I agreed to. Agreed? Suggested. Ever since I read the Gor books (yes, yes I did, so what?) I've been fantasizing about being branded. A mark burned into my body that says I'm his. More his than a ring can say, or collar, or even a tattoo with a heart and arrow and his name inked into my skin in the tacky environment of a tattoo parlor by a hairy guy named Big Ed.

We've talked about the branding, my lover and I, read Web pages, decided on the brand, bought supplies to keep the branding from getting infected. Now it's time, and I wanted the whole experience. I wanted to be tied, gagged, and helpless. Remember the old saying, *be careful what you wish for*? I am tied, gagged, blindfolded, helpless, no safe word or grunt or gesture. I am going to have a brand like some cow in the pasture, only my skin isn't leather and I know what the smell of burning metal means and even though I went to the bathroom before he tied me, my bladder feels full. Sweat is pouring from my skin in droplets, soaking the bed.

He is standing over me, the cool alcohol swab feeling so good against my flushed skin. I am hot, it's the sweaty heat of absolute terror. Isn't this what I wanted, always pushing, always wanting more—more pain, more fear, his cock punishing me, ramming inside my throat, my unlubricated ass? Now I'm getting more, more than I can handle. I don't want to do this, the problem is, what I want doesn't matter. I have no way of screaming stop, the screams and whimpers and "NO, NO" coming out of my ball gag as incomprehensible sounds that could be pleasure. There is no backing out, and I am helpless and afraid and I wonder if I'll pee the bed or pass out, I'm hoping for passing out.

The smell of metal is getting stronger, I can hear the fire popping. We chose to leave our house and rent a cabin in the woods. That way no one would call the fire department or any other potentially embarrassing thing. I didn't realize the potential embarrassment would be internal. I am going to shame myself because I finally found a limit, only, it's too late.

I have to be honest, in spite of the terror and discovery of a limit, the knots in my stomach are not all fear. No, there is the sexual tingling of finally discovering true helplessness. Poor lover, can never really rape me or beat me into oblivion because I always really want it. I don't want this, but I'm going to get it, and that total helplessness has me so turned on I could come with the simplest touch. Only the touch I'm about to get isn't the kind I need.

I hear him walking to the fire, he is telling me what he is doing. "Pet, I'm walking to the fire, pulling out the brand, it's glowing red." He is talking softly, gently, about his red hot poker, and I'm thinking I'm going to puke. Great, now I have three choices, puke, wet myself, or pass out. A few minutes ago I thought I had no choices at all. "I'm standing over you now. I'm going to mark you as mine." He is purring, his brand of ownership to always be on my body, burned in my skin. I am screaming, my throat hurts, my head feels as if it might explode. I'm thinking a stroke isn't a far-fetched possibility; I'm not sure my body can hold such fear, such excitement.

I feel the heat before it comes close to my hip. I can picture the glowing red of the silver brand. Closer, closer, then pain. I am trying to struggle, but he has me tied really well, my lover knows his ropes. I am screaming but all that is coming from behind the gag is whimpers. I am sobbing, my tears mingling with the sweat pouring down my face. He is counting the seconds we decided on to make the brand permanent, I can barely hear him over the roaring in my ears. I don't think I will pass out from the pain. I can't describe it, do justice to the pain, but I'll try: It's intense, and it is the focal point of my life. I can feel my muscles bunched, knotted like the rope tying me down. My fists are clenched, heart pounding, and I am taking the pain. I have no choice as my hip burns and blackens and blisters. I think he's stopped counting and the branding iron is gone, but it doesn't matter because it still burns, still hurts. I can feel his hand touching between the folds of my lips, and yes I'm wet, yes I'm excited. Even through the pain I can feel his fingers probing inside of me, and I know I am going to orgasm. I don't want to, I feel I've given everything I have to give and he wants more; I'm limp and ragged and my hip hurts.

Still, he wants something more, and it's something I can give him, because I can feel the coiling in my belly that tells me my orgasm is close. Suddenly my body stiffens, and I scream into the gag, only this time in pleasure. When my orgasm finally subsides, he removes his hand. I feel his body weight press down on the bed in front of me, his cock pressing between my legs. He can only enter me shallowly, from in front, my legs are tied together but I'm wet enough that he can glide over my thighs and between my wet swollen lips. Belly to belly, I can feel his cock gliding in and out, his hands trailing along my body, feeling the sweat, the heat. His fingers stop right before the brand, my breath catches, I feel him gently trace his brand, barely touching, but the pain makes me squirm, the squirming pushing me closer to him. I feel his thrusting increase, and I know I'm going to come with him, as he suddenly grabs my hips, his fingers digging into the muscles of my bottom, the weight of his wrist against my brand making me scream and wiggle harder. I can feel him coming, the sticky wetness on my thighs and lips, my own orgasm answering him. We lay there a moment, panting. I know he will soon untie me, ask me if I am okay. I also know I will probably laugh, and tell him about the rush, the high, and not mention I wanted him to stop. My reputation as a pain slut will stay firmly in place. In fact, I'm already wondering if we shouldn't put a matching brand on my left hip.

BETHLEHEM'S BURNING

Eve Rings

Miss Rhode Island considers herself in the mirror, picking a piece of spinach from between her teeth, a stowaway from this afternoon's salad at the Holiday Inn. She reapplies her Apricot Bliss lipstick, smoothing her dress over her stomach, wondering if she looks bloated from the two iced teas with artificial lemon she had with lunch. She blots her mouth as she hears a knock on the door. Adjusting her tiara, she answers it on teetering heels.

"You have five minutes. He's paid an extra fifty to fuck you up the ass."

She picks her glittery sash off the piss-stained couch, a wreath of wilted roses in her arms. Friday nights are always two-for-one.

The corridor is bright, white cement floor, white fluorescent lights, white walls and white moths that fly into them, smashing their papery bodies against plaster, translucent wings littering the floor like snowflakes. In front of Door Three stands Headless, the door open a crack and her in front of it, looking inside and gesturing to Miss Rhode Island with a finger placed over her tremendous lips.

"Who's The Swamper tonight?"

They peer into the dimly lit room, shoulders huddled together and breathing hushed as they watch the girl crawling across the floor, her body encased in thick yellow rubber. Her tongue is pink behind the puckered synthetic of her face mask, and she licks the floor as a man sits on the red velvet loveseat, his eyes half-closed in ecstasy. Flies sizzle across the gummy puddles on the carpet, steam rising from the ground and the wallpaper peeling off. Headless gives a mock shiver, stepping back from the door and softly shutting it.

"Thank God it's Friday. I really fucking hate Tuesdays. On Tuesdays, Headless has to be The Swamper."

She squeezes Miss Rhode Island's shoulder and walks down the hallway to Door Seven, where the plywood and the basket await her, strategically placed mirrors and Karo syrup blood, a man with $300 less in his wallet. Miss Rhode Island consults a clipboard hanging from the wall, even though she knows she has the auditorium, scanning the xeroxed papers with a perfectly manicured crimson nail, rehearsing her acceptance speech, even though it's heart-memorized by six months. She reads that Door Five is occupied by The Trunk, and since they were redecorating the stables, Bethlehem was now in Room Twelve, which had been swathed with blue silk sheets and straw on the floor. Girls like The Trunk make the most money, because they had actually signed a contract, agreed to the modifications being made to them, some even suggesting the changes, like The Pin. The Trunk made $800 a session, which The House took twenty percent of, a small price for the limbs she had removed. The House had considered finding their own amputee, but most of the women they interviewed weren't attractive enough for the position. The Trunk was usually kept in the same room except on cleaning days, and she had a regular clientele who bought her gifts; huge, lacy heart shaped boxes of candy and perfume in gallon jugs. She didn't get out much. Some of the girls chose to live at The House, others had their own apartments. Bethlehem was always Bethlehem. Beth, as everyone called her, was so used to the crucifixion that her wounds had remained open for the last six years, bleeding only when she was moved to epiphany or her stigmata acted up, which was rare these days.

The House tried to encourage her visions, once even sending her to Rome, because they could always charge double if the spirit moved her. The irony of most of her customers being excommunicated priests wasn't lost on Beth, and she considered her job a sort of sacred public service. She would have been a nun if she wasn't a whore. Miss Rhode Island makes her way to the auditorium, her heels crushing the wings of flies under blazing patent leather.

The room is large, set up with twenty or so tables, white tablecloths and pink and blue carnations, sprays of baby's breath in cheap plastic vases. Glittering silver disco lights hang from the ceiling, casting snags of light across the floor, the stage with the red faux velvet carpet crawling down the runway. The room can accommodate up to two hundred guests if all the tables are set up, but tonight's audience was one, the ember of his cigarette sparking in the dimly lit room, his feet propped up on the table. Miss Rhode Island quietly steps behind the curtain, making her way backstage, adjusting her garters under her tight-fitting gown. She hits the button on the stereo, Bert Parks flooding the strategically placed speakers, her footsteps graceful as she makes her entrance, her hand waving stiffly as tears roll down her cheeks. She walks to the end of the platform, smiling to her imaginary audience, clutching her decaying roses to her chest, waiting for the song to end. The room falls silent. Raising her lips to the microphone, she makes her acceptance speech.

"I am so thrilled, a dream has come true. I am deeply grateful to the judges and I know the folks at home are so excited. During my reign I plan to do my best to serve you, my adoring public, and to end the energy crisis and solve world hunger."

Her audience stands, unzipping his dirty jeans and taking out his cock. Spitting in his hand, he approaches the stage.

"Get on your knees."

Miss Rhode Island does what the customer orders, the beads on her dress shimmering as she hikes it over her hips.

"Your skin, it's so warm."

She looks down at him, his head bent at her feet, his papery mouth covering her skin in dry kisses, ferocious and chaste at once, the feel of his hands gripping her ankles. She looks to the ceiling, her head shorn yet crowned with barbed wire and dried flowers, the dried wings of the moths from the hallway, anything she could find that matched the depictions she had seen, from black velvet oil paintings and the stained glass she remembered from ancient churches.

"You're burning up. I think we should take you down."

He starts to reach for the nails, his hands scraping against the rotting wood.

She looks to an unseen voice and answers, her voice the smallest whisper.

"Not yet."

Death lays in Room Four, holding an Eternal Rest Tribute over her chest, her skin dusted pale blue and her lips white. Candles burn in huge wrought iron holders, wax dripping on the heavily polished wood floor, organ music piped in over the cheap sound system. She has practiced slowing her breath, her chest barely rising with each exhale, her slight intakes inaudible. The room is heavily air conditioned and the toe tag itches, yet her eyes remain closed, her body glowing against the satin lined coffin. The House told her the more realistic she is, the better her tips will be, but she has a difficult time keeping her face impassive when the customers begin to cry.

She counts, backwards from one thousand, her mind blank

to anything but the numbers, the simple language of digits. She thinks of going back to Kansas to her family, the feel of the solid metal tractor against her face as she rests her cheek against it, the miasmatic stench of sugar beets. She feels the tears hot across her naked thighs, salty splashes of grief, warm mouth lowered to lick them off, the slow stream of saliva across her skin. She feels his weight on top of her as he climbs into the coffin, his body hard and warm against her dormant flesh, his scorching mouth covering hers as he worms his tongue between her lips. She is dead weight as he spreads her legs, her limbs heavy and laggard. Her eyes open as the screaming begins in Room Nine.

Nurse Johnson stands over the body, her hands flapping around her face, red lips open in a hysterical shriek, fingers flying over her mouth then off again, swatting at the air. The man is naked, his bloated white belly paler than the rest of him, which is a flush of pink. A hypodermic is lodged in his arm and his mouth is open, his fat puffy tongue trying to escape the trap of his lips. Doors are opened and people rush in, some hardly dressed, others wrapped in bed sheets and towels. The Nurse just points, still screaming until The Pin leads her to the gurney, pushing her down and shushing her.

"What happened?"

The Nurse opens her mouth, her lips forming words but no sounds, just ragged gasps and her wet sniffles.

"Fuck, he must have had a heart attack."

The House runs in, damage control, telling everyone to go see the front desk for refunds and that they were closing for the night. The Pin considers the damage, watches as The House checks the body, covering it with a sheet, digging in the discarded pants for the wallet and littering the floor with identification and plastic credit cards.

"I'm gonna take The Nurse back to my room and get her changed."

The House nods, scratching his stubble riddled chin, shrugging and hoisting the body onto his shoulders. The Pin takes The Nurse by the elbow and leads her to her room, her latex skirt making slurping noises as she walks.

Miss Rhode Island walks down the white hallway, her tiara in one hand and her shoes in the other, her lipstick smudged, glittery orange over her chin. She stops in front of The Pin, who has her arm around The Nurse, The Pin shining under the bright lights, her numerous facial piercings reflecting tiny prisms across the walls.

"Long night, huh? God, I hate Fridays. The House said they are considering stopping the two-fer's because we get too much business and… hey, what's up?"

The Nurse sniffled and The Pin shook her head, her jewelry tinkling together like tinny metal alarms.

"Her customer bit it. We're gonna go change."

Miss Rhode Island frowns and passes them, her words thrown over her shoulder.

"Meet you outside."

The Nurse strips off her latex costume, spitting on a

Kleenex and rubbing it across her eyes, black kohl smudged on white tissue and her back-seamed stockings pulled off and thrown over a chair. She dresses like The Pin when not at work, jeans and a T-shirt, her hair pulled into a ponytail and her feet in dirty sneakers. The Pin looks at her, removing the leather collar from around her throat, pulling white socks on over her feet, metal rings and implants vanishing behind cotton.

"You okay?"

"Yeah. I think so. Am I gonna be in trouble?"

The Pin shakes her head, her jewelry clanking together.

"Nah. The House made him sign the waiver. Your ass is covered."

"Fuck, he had a wife and kids… I mean, Jesus…," The Nurse looks up to see Bethlehem at the door, her body barely covered in a slip of white burlap, the edges dirty with blood. Her voice is soft.

"Someone died here tonight."

"One of my clients."

Beth nods and leaves the room, her footfalls soundless.

The Pin grabs a coat off the bed. "Let's go."

The parking lot is a mass of screeching tires and headlights, and Miss Rhode Island sits on the hill overlooking the mobile panic, her knees pulled to her chest, the stars pricking the night sky. She hears the animals in the stable, the bleating of the lamb and the two chickens, the cow The House had bought from a farm that was in foreclosure, rescuing him from the dog food factory. She watches as The Nurse and The Pin climb the hill, The Nurse with her arms wrapped tightly around her shoulders, probably contemplating what questions the police will interrogate her with when they show up after The House makes the mandatory 911 call.

"What happened?" Miss Rhode Island looks at her, brushing a stray lock of hair that had snarled its way into her mouth.

The Nurse sits down heavily with a sigh. "I don't know. He wanted the usual, for me to give him his medicine. You've been Nurse, you've done it before."

"Maybe an air bubble got into the needle." The Pin offers her theory, stretching her legs in front of her, picking the blood-bloated body of a mosquito off her perforated arm.

"Maybe he was just too old." Miss Rhode Island looks to The House sees the shade go up in Room Twelve, votive candles shinning softly behind the dismal window.

"Maybe he deserved to die." The Nurse closes her eyes, resting her head on her arm, her hair covering her face like a blonde shadow.

"Maybe everything does." And as the words dissolve from Miss Rhode Island's mouth, they see Bethlehem go up in flames, like a prayer.

CRASH 97

Kevin Lano

The damaged cars triggered a sexual reverie of increasing violence. He watched as the police pulled open the crumpled doors of the Laguna, thrown sideways by the impact across the incoming traffic lanes at the entrance to the vehicle tunnel. Blood was sprayed across the inside surface of the fractured glass, but the occupants were still hidden inside the car behind the shadow of the tunnel. C joined him silently at the office window as he stared intently down at the gathering ritual of death. The central terminal area was now cut off from the outside world as the chaos and congestion caused by the crash built up.

Afterwards as he drives her home he endlessly re-explores the details of the injuries they had witnessed, contrasting the choreography of this minor accident to the high-speed collision of Diana Spencer's limousine with a Paris motorway pillar. *Carried from the car, blood saturated her white dress, dripping in a line all the way to the ambulance.* She was still moving. *So was Diana apparently—lying mutilated for hours in the wreckage before they freed her to die.*

Unlike the other managers at Heathrow, who were old ex-public school men of mind-numbing predictability, he triggered for her an explicit recapitulation of the sense of impending disaster that hung over the airport. Permanently on the edge of crisis, it seemed a zone of unreality that progressed each day closer to physical and psychological breakdown. After taking part in a staging of a mock accident, she continually imagined the after-effects of a genuine air crash into a terminal: The serried rows of bloody corpses laid out with blank identification tags on the concrete aprons; the mangled steel geometry of the planes and buildings burning into the night sky; the thousands of disoriented passengers and frantic relatives.

Leaving the Westway he begins to explore the wound areas of her genitals and thighs under her dress; a history of love and atrocities memorialized in these irregular scars. She stares ahead, watching the brake lights of the vehicles flare in the reflection of the wet tarmac-like pools of luminous blood.

Parking in the churchyard beside her house he wordlessly grapples with her aroused body, forcing his penis into her rectum, probing rapidly in and out as she grimaces with pain. In front of his eyes he still sees the twisted corpses being hauled from the crash, and remains disconnected from her.

She feels that he reduces her to just a physical object, a collection of orifices and responses; but realizes that this is what she has been seeking at a certain level—this seems the only thing that is reliable and real.

On her first visit to his flat he shows her his collection of photographs of deformed genitalia, and this sets the tone for their future relationship. Solicited through adverts in gay and men's magazines, these grotesque images of mutated and intersex organs could raise either a response of disgust or humor. As always, he interprets them as a question "Just how would you deal with them? What techniques would you use? Could these things lead to entirely new ways of having sex or conceptualizing its meaning—that is the key issue."

His endgame obsessions with the breakdown of reality, the crash photographs of Diana, conspiracy theories into Ian Curtis' death, the meaning of Denis Nilsen's killings, at first disturbed her, then began to fit an underlying logic she recognized in her own fears.

Under photographs of Cambodian atrocities, cairns of severed heads, temples burning in deserted cities, he stabs his penis between the inflamed lips of her labia, seeking some new intersection or wound.

He took her on one of his regular trips to the crash site in Paris.

Already this seemed to have become a covert pilgrimage for many people, with local service stations selling Diana mementos to the tourists who came to hunt out the disappearing traces of the collision. Even as they parked by the underpass there was another car ahead of them with a couple filming the enigmatic intersecting lines, which marked this death.

He drives repeatedly through the tunnel, trying to exactly follow the last movements of the speeding car, his own private reconstruction of the multiple collisions and fatal trajectory of the heavy Mercedes.

On the way back he fucks her in the terminal posture of the princess, drawing lines of her menstrual blood on her face and breasts as she lays limply twisted in the back seat in imitation of a corpse.

"The crash, and the extreme reaction to it, reveals a desire for the end of civilization, an abolition of the narrow codes of everyday existence. It was the first time for years that many people had experienced any genuine feelings."

She realizes that he is trying in some way to resurrect the princess; he tells her that he sees Diana all the time abandoned in her tomb, weeping alone through the cold nights.

He gets her to dress like Diana and imitate her make-up and hairstyle.

He sodomizes her in the back of the car, paying a prostitute to lick out her cunt as he holds her scarred and naked body contorted as if after a crash, folded between the collapsed surfaces of a concertinad vehicle. As the girl's teeth closed on her clit, she shuddered in a rictus of orgasm or excavation, rectum contracting around the hard pole of his cock, attempting to expel it from her body.

Her premonitions of an incipient holocaust increased. From the runways the planes lifted into the sky at two-minute intervals, an endless replication of annihilation.

Watching from his car parked by the perimeter road she realizes he has begun to live out his psychotic dreams, a return to the primitive, a disintegration of all meaning.

In this real world of emptiness only the killing made sense. When he returned to the car she put her hand in his lap; there was blood there. "Some accident," he said. As his hands grasped the wheel she noticed more blood under his fingernails.

A GIRL ON THE TRAIN

Sonia Greenfield

She gets on the subway at the college and sits across from you. You face each other, one on either side of the doors. When you look up from your lap, she makes eye contact, and then you look away; when she looks up from her lap and you make eye contact she looks away, out of the window at the passing buildings, as the late day sun falls across her face in a bar of orange light. When your eyes meet again a minute or so later, she smiles slightly, looks at her bag, and pulls a book out.

She would be reading Baudelaire, untranslated, if she opened the book, but instead she watches the walls of the tunnel that the train has just passed into. When the train arrives at the next station, you watch each other through the new passengers that board until the space gets filled and your view is blocked by the torsos of German tourists.

You could not know this, but ten minutes before she

boarded the train she was masturbating in the college library, on the fifth floor, in the children's section—back against the yellow spines of Nancy Drew books, index finger expertly circling her clit. It was the excitement of the dentist appointment that she is on her way to now. Her face is flushed.

She presses her tongue against the broken tooth and with each application of pressure a sharp sensation of nervy pain shoots through her mouth and she likes it. A lot. She presses her fingers into the bruise on her thigh and the double sensation of the acute stabbing in her mouth and the dull throbbing in her thigh almost makes her come right there, across from you.

You catch a glimpse of her catching a glimpse of you and you smile.

In her mind she is replaying certain memories that resurface occasionally. If you could read her thoughts, you would see her being felt up by the school janitor when she was twelve. The garage cluttered with rags, oilcans, and bicycle parts, his hand up her shirt, rubbing across her anthill breasts, the nipples just starting to swell. He was showing her pictures in a magazine—shots of older men squirting semen on the bellies of seven-year-old girls.

You would also see her finding her dead dog twisted in the bushes where it landed after her father kicked it off the back porch which was two-stories high. The drunken rages. Steel-toed boots.

Hiding in the closet in third grade with Roxanne. Roxanne asking her if she wanted to know what rape felt like and then letting her grope her body in the dark until Allison opened the door and found them. Roxanne's hand down the front of her panties. Word spreading through school. Dirty. Slut.

You could see Bobby putting her mother's head through the glass door.

You would see Jeff forcing her to suck his cock.

You see her through the tourists again now that the people on the train have thinned out. She is staring off into space—somewhere above and to the right of your head.

You might see the nights spent at S/M clubs—having electrical tape ripped off of her nipples. You might see her forcing her fist into the cunt of a woman strapped to the wall.

You don't. If you had been able to see her thoughts you might have been tempted to feel sorry for her, and this sentiment of pity, this belief of yours that you could comfort her in some way, would be a waste. Because, in truth, she enjoys these little memories and those buried even deeper within her subconscious. She plays them out for pleasure. Each memory is like a broken tooth with a tongue pressing into the jagged space.

She stands up and slings her bag onto her shoulder. It is a red backpack. Her shoes are brown and polished to a soft gleam and she wears a gray skirt and a white blouse, one button opened exposing a small triangle of pale skin just below her neck. You study the line of her body as she waits for the train to stop. This is where she gets off. The train pulls into the station and the doors open. She walks off toward the escalator going up, her ponytail swinging with each step and you think to yourself as you watch her disappear—"Why can't I meet a nice girl like that?"

CHENG

Cara Bruce

Cheng gave the phrase two-faced a whole new meaning. After his fame from his appearance on *Ripley's Believe It Or Not* he had traveled to Hollywood and worked for a while, getting small cameo parts, anytime there was a freak or a weirdo needed he was called. But there were only so many requests for a man with two mouths and after the craze wore off he couldn't even get a part in a commercial. His agent stopped returning his calls and he was no longer invited to any of the parties.

His lease ran up and Cheng was out on the streets, forced into residential hotels that stunk of the sweet smell of crack. No one cared for a dried up old freak and the welfare checks never lasted long enough. It's okay to be weird when you're popular, but there's nothing worse then being strange and a has-been.

Once in a while the stray tourist would recognize him, doing a double take as they wandered wide-eyed down Hollywood or Santa Monica Boulevard. Not only did Cheng have two mouths but he was short as well. If it weren't for his suddenly grotesque deformity he would now be a regular little person, eligible for all sorts of movie parts. There was always need for a midget, a dwarf or an otherwise vertically challenged individual.

Cheng's days were empty and lonely. How he longed for the paparazzi, the bright lights of the tabloid photographers as he scampered from one hot tub to the next. That had been the life. He picked up the pile of food stamps that held nothing but the promise of government cheese. Stuff for the poor, the untalented; the normal.

Sitting in a coffee shop on Santa Monica Boulevard, tapping his fingers under the green fluorescent lights of the dingy diner, Cheng looked out of the window into the hot L.A. night. Boys. Tons of them. Boys dressed like girls. Boys in tiny tight shorts, boys in boots with white tank tops. Boys falling over each other, hanging on the open windows of cars, loitering on street corners.

Cheng hadn't noticed Simon until he slid into the booth across from him. Simon didn't say a word, emptying a pink packet of Sweet & Low into his cup and stirring.

His very presence made Cheng acutely uncomfortable. Simon made the diner even dirtier, dropping everything to a more depressing level. But, was it better for him to be alone or to have a friend, a companion? These were the kind of questions Cheng had hoped never to be asking.

The city was closing in on him. Cheng cleared his throat, attempting to dislodge anything at all. His mind drifted to the desert, to a sky so dark you could actually see the stars. Things would be easier there. Or at least cheaper.

"How's life treating you?" Simon asked, hand paused, eyes lifted.

"Alright," Cheng said, adding a nonchalant shrug to his shoulders.

"Hmm," Simon let out a slight cough, pursed his lips and nodded his head. "Well, I'm glad to hear that," he said, "Real glad to hear you're not looking for work or anything."

Cheng flicked his tongue over his chapped lips, letting out a nervous laugh, "Work? Hell, a man's always looking for work."

Simon nodded again, raising his eyes. "Acting?"

"Not at the moment," Cheng answered.

"Auditioning?"

"Not really."

"On call?"

Cheng fidgeted in his seat. Simon was fucking with him. Simon knew his time had come and gone. Cheng pulled himself up to his full height. He didn't have to put up with this crap from some two-bit sleaze.

"I got a proposition for you," Simon said.

"What's that?"

"I have a couple of friends coming to town. They want to see some freaky stuff, real L.A. stuff they say. They want to meet a star. Have a good time. I was thinking you could take them out."

"Like to dinner?"

"Sure. Wherever. Anyplace you want to go. These men have a lot of money."

"There's Spago and Mezza Luna," Cheng was beginning to get a little excited. This would be fun. A night out on the town in places where he could be seen. That was probably all that he needed, for those that had forgotten about him to see him again. Once they remembered his magnificent two mouths, they would be all over him. After all, Halloween was just around the corner.

"Yeah, right." Simon was looking around, his eyes flitting distractedly over everyone in the joint, "My friends have special needs, Cheng."

"Needs? What, are they kosher, vegetarian, diabetic?"

"Not quite. See, those places for dinner are fine and all but I was thinking more about you being their companion for the night, if you catch my drift."

The words sunk in as Cheng sat back. Simon's words delivered a stinging smack across his face.

"Why me?" Cheng heard his own voice, sounding a million miles away, so tiny and so lost.

"Why you?" Simon laughed, a bellowing laugh that shot through the air and bounced off every formica table and cracked coffee cup. "Cheng, my dear friend, because you are a freak. You can do them both at once. My god, look at you, you could make millions as a john. You're young, attractive, slightly famous, and you have two mouths. You could make twice as much as all the other guys."

Simon sat back and looked at him. Cheng felt a blush run up his face, he had never thought of that. Of actually using his double lipped face for anything but acting. He couldn't say that the thought repulsed him, but if anyone ever found out... why, he would never work in this town again.

The run of emotions and ideas quickly played across Cheng's double visage. Simon watched and waited for the perfect time to seal the deal. Brows furrowed, face tensed, then relaxed.

"Five hundred bucks for each of them, one thousand to spend the entire night."

Cheng let his mouths drop. With that money he'd be able to pay off his debts and get himself back on his feet, no problem. He'd get to go out for a nice dinner, be seen with these men, and then get paid. And for what? A double blow job? Cheng had never been with a man, he had never expected to. To tell the truth he had never even thought about it. Sure, he didn't have the best luck with women but even that hadn't made him think about men.

Surprisingly, the thought did not disgust him.

"Well?" Simon was waiting.

Cheng looked into the almost empty brownish black coffee filling his cup. There was something in the way he had used too much half-and-half that told him his life was over anyway. It was too milky, too creamy, and too light.

"Okay," he said, "I'll do it."

The next evening Cheng dressed with anticipation. The emotion scared him. For the first time in his life he doubted his heterosexuality. He dressed in jeans, cowboy boots and a tight shirt that he tucked in. He didn't want to look like one of the trampy street boys but he did want to look sexy.

The buzzer rang and with a final glance in the mirror he hurried downstairs. The man who had gotten out of the car was good looking, a collared shirt, gelled hair. He smiled when he saw Cheng, lifted a hand and placed it gently on his face turning him around, looking at one mouth then the other.

"Perfect," he whispered.

Cheng focused on the palm tree swaying above his head to make sure it wasn't a cutout. Real life was so hard to believe. He let the man open the door to the black Lexus and slid in, hands resting on the leather interior.

The man driving turned around and smiled at him as well. Both of these men were undeniably attractive. The men drove in silence and Cheng said nothing. He watched the lights from the highway bounce against the windshield and wondered if they found him at all appealing.

A clinking shock brought them from the quiet night of outside into the clanging glasses and laughter of the trendy Santa Monica eatery. The restaurant was crowded. Beautiful, slender waiters maneuvered through linen-covered tables, china plates held on sky-turned palms. Cheng puffed himself up to a full three feet five and surveyed the scene. The men had picked the restaurant and he had never been here before. The place was full of men, each one more gorgeous then the last—shining hair, bright white smiles. Perfectly toned bodies could be traced under impeccably tailored Armani suits. Everyone stopped to watch as Cheng and his companions were led through the maze of tables. Self-consciousness was biting at the back of his neck as he wandered through seat after seat of Adonises. As he passed each table the men would pause, fork raised to mouth or glass raised in toast. Each of them looked at the dwarfish freak with a look that Cheng was unfamiliar with—lust.

They were seated in the center of the restaurant. Cheng tried to start conversations a couple of times but the men weren't interested in small talk.

The waiter came by and the two men ordered for themselves, dinners of foie gras and salmon. Cheng opened the one mouth connected to the voice box and began to order his own meal but the waiter smiled politely and turned his back mid-sentence.

"What about me?" Cheng asked.

The taller man laughed, "We want you hungry."

Cheng was about to speak when the lights went off. The faint sound of chairs scraping across the floor could be heard and men clearing their throats. Cheng's heart was pounding in his chest, his breath strangling in his esophagus. Something was terribly wrong. Suddenly a spotlight beamed onto his table, the two men were nowhere to be found. The maitre d' was standing in front of him with a microphone.

"Brothers," he said, "Tonight we bring you something very special. A sexual freak of nature so extraordinary, so unbelievable, that your cocks will be rock hard in your pants in no time." The eruption of hearty laughter forced Cheng to focus on the crowd in the darkness. The bright white smiles were illuminated by the spotlight causing the men to look both sinister and happy. The room began to spin and Cheng felt faint. The announcer spread out his hands towards Cheng, "Who is going to be the first to step right up and greet our new friend?"

Cheng felt a pair of fingers opening up his extra mouth. He shut his eyes as another pair of hands smoothed back his hair. He recognized the voice of the man who had driven him and he let himself relax. He had never been the center of this sort of attention.

Cheng leaned back as the man's cock pushed into his mouth, going straight for the back of his throat. He felt another hard dick entering his second pair of lips. The two cocks rubbed against each other with nothing but a thin wall of the skin of his face separating them.

Cheng felt himself getting hard. Someone was unbuttoning his pants. A circle of men stood around him, watching the performance. Cocks were springing out of dress pants, jeans and khakis. Men were beating off around him. A mouth enveloped his own prick, moving up and down over the veiny member, applying hard suction. Cheng had once paid a woman for a blow job but it was nothing like this. This man knew what he was doing. He decided to concentrate on the dick in his face. He began trying, applying pressure, and using his tongue. The other mouth he had no control over. He could do nothing but let the mouth be used however the man wanted to, he was all at once conscious of how much smaller it was.

He felt the first man growing very stiff in his mouth as he suddenly grabbed Cheng's head and blasted. Cheng panicked. He had never had come shot down his throat and wondered if he should spit or swallow. Under the excitement of one man coming the other did as well. But he pulled out and jerked himself to orgasm, his come puddling on the floor. Cheng was being covered. Men were surrounding him, brushing dicks against his head, his mouths; he fell in and out of orgasmic consciousness. He came not once, but twice, and lost count of how many lips were on his dick. Then, all of a sudden, it was over.

He was exhausted and lay back in his chair. Strong arms were around him, lifting him up and carrying him. He was laid down upon a velveteen couch, drifting quickly off to sleep.

He awoke hours later in darkness. Fear overtook him, the night and its viscious memories came creeping back. Fumbling through the blackness he found a light switch. Surprisingly he was dressed and alone. An envelope lay on the couch. Cheng opened it and pulled out the note.

Thanks for everything.

In addition to this were one hundred crisp 100-dollar bills.

Cheng left the restaurant and stood on the corner to hail a cab. He breathed in the hot, heavy air of the Los Angeles night, clenching his tiny fist tightly around the bills. He lay back against the torn vinyl taxi seats and reflected on his life. His acting career, his welfare checks, his loneliness and last night. $10,000 was enough to start over. He didn't have to live here and hope someone would ever appreciate him. He would go where people would have respect, where he could make money. He would be a king.

"Driver," he said, "how much to Las Vegas?"

CONTRIBUTORS

Dani Bauter is a writer in her mid-twenties living in San Francisco. She is the Assistant Editor of Venus or Vixen? and the owner of the copyediting business Check Yourself. Her writing has been published on www.venusorvixen.com and she is anxiously awaiting the time when she can retire from her day job and write for a living.

David Beran lives in Los Angeles and writes screenplays, short stories and radio dramas. His interests include horror films, old-time radio, World's Fairs, and King Ludwig II's grottos.

m.i. blue writes, performs, and produces shows in San Francisco. He has produced the weird and successful wordfuck and dadafest series and stories for *Future Sex* and *Noirotica 2*, as well as the informational pamphlet "How To Blow Up A Church."

Paul Bradshaw is an English writer whose influences include Christopher Priest, Poppy Z Brite, and H P Lovecraft. He has had over sixty short story acceptances in the UK and USA, and is currently editor of *The Dream Zone*, a quarterly collection of imaginative fiction.

M. Christian's work has appeared in such books as *Best American Erotica*, *Best Gay Erotica*, *The Mammoth Books of Erotica* series (International, New, Historical, and Short Erotic Novels), and many, many other anthologies and magazines. He is the editor of the anthologies *Eros Ex Machina*, *Midsummer Night's Dreams*, *Guilty Pleasures*, and (with Simon Sheppard) *Rough Stuff: Tales of Gay Men, Sex and Power*. A collection of his short stories, *Dirty Words*, will be published next year from Alyson Books.

Heather Corinna is the editor and founder of *Scarlet Letters: A Journal of Femmerotica*, and is a sex correspondent for *SheWire*, *Maxi*, *LeisureSuit.Net* and other publications. Her written work is appearing in several anthologies this year and is produced in a variety of online venues. She works as a freelance writer, editor, designer, exotic model and all-around professional Pop Tart.

Patty Cursed is a 25-year-old San Francisco based writer. She believes some things should be left to the imagination.

W. Bill Czolgosz works as a trapper and a bootlegger in Saskatchewan. When he visits the city, he wears fur and doesn't care if you object. He is currently working on a memoir about life in *Winterville* and a historical sex novella called *Frontier Whore*.

Blag Dahlia is a San Francisco record producer and founder of the notorious punk band The Dwarves. His first novel *Armed to the Teeth with Lipstick* won the Newberry Children's Book Award for inspiring night sweats and bed-wetting.

Sue D'Nimm is a former parapsychologist. She has published one book, *Nature of Mind*, and has been published in many small presses, including, *Mindmares, Apparitions,* and *Cabal Asylum*. She currently works as a psychologist.

Astrid Fox's most recent erotic novel is *Rika's Jewel*, a Xenaesque Viking fantasy described by *Diva Magazine* as "Splendid Stuff!" Current naughty collections publishing her work include *Sugar & Spice 2*, *Wicked Words* and *The Mammoth Book of Lesbian Erotica*. She writes under a variety of pseudonyms and hails originally from depraved small-town Alaska.

When **Sonia Greenfield** is not writing about messed-up people, who, not so coincidently, happen to be her very-best-favorite kind of people, she can be found in a cubicle, ruining her eyes, back and wrists working for the computer industry. She has been published in *14 Hills*, *Flux*, *Crack* and *Mirage #4 Period(ical)*.

A vocalist, musician, songwriter, and arranger with Swans for 13 years, **Jarboe** has released 4 solo albums, 19 albums with Swans and related projects, and numerous collaborative projects worldwide. Her fifth album, *Disburden Disciple,* slated for December 99 contains material recorded in Israel and will carry a multimedia presentation and links to her Web site: TheLivingJarboe.com.
Jarboe@mindspring.com
Box 420232, Atlanta GA 30342

Jeremiah Juarez was born and has enjoyably spent the majority of his life in Los Angeles. From being born into the Jehovah's Witness occult to discovering the beauty and unity of the dance culture/movement, Jerry works to live until he wins the Lotto.

Rebecca Kissel has been happily married to her lover, Jim, for 17 years. Jim was a naval officer and she accompanied him all over the U.S. and Korea, before finally settling down in the hot sultry south.

Kevin Lano lives in London, UK, and has written and edited a number of books on gender and sexuality, including *Breaking the Barriers to Desire* (Five Leaves Press, 1995) and *Beyond Sexuality* (Phoenix Press, 1992). He has been active in the lesbian, gay and bisexual communities for many years, and is currently editing a collection of bisexual erotica.

Lydia Lunch has appeared on over 70 CDs, in 20 films, has written 6 books, exhibits her photography and sculpture and tours the world, all to further explore her ongoing obsession with confronting the apathy and bullshit which defines the status quo.

Carol Queen has a doctorate in sex, and she worked very hard on her labs. She is the author of *The Leather Daddy and the Femme*, *Real Live Nude Girl*, and *Exhibitionism for the Shy*.

Amy Rasmussen has her dark side house-trained; the sick stuff mostly comes out to play on paper.

Eve Rings has had her work published in numerous places. Her story *The Cannibal's Daughter* has been suggested for a year 2000 Stoker award. "The Porcelain God," a chapbook co-authored with Joi Brozek, is available from Blindside Press. She loves trash culture, loud music, shoes and her son. Check out her Web site: http://www.magdaleneandthemarquis.com/Whore.

Thomas S. Roche's writing has appeared in such horror and erotica anthologies as *Love in Vein 2*, the *Hot Blood* series, the *Best American Erotica* series, and many others. His short story collections include *Sucker Punches* (Blue Blood Books) and *Dark Matter* (Masquerade Books). He has recently finished his first novel, *Violent Angel*.

Michelle Scalise has sold over 100 poems and short stories to such magazines as *Pirate Writings*, *Talebones*, *Epitaph*, *Edgar*, *Roadworks*, *Eternity*, *Mindmares*, *Gentlemen's Cabaret* and *Voices and Verses*.

Simon Sheppard is the co-editor, with M. Christian, of *Rough Stuff: Tales of Gay Men, Sex, and Power*. His stories appear in dozens of anthologies, including *The Best American Erotica 2000, Best Gay Erotica 2000*, *Bending the Landscape: Horror*, and *Sexcrime*. Thanks to Thomas Roche for the twisted impetus.

Cecilia Tan has been writing smut since she was a teenager, when, not coincidentally, she read a lot of science fiction. She founded Circlet Press, publishers of erotic science fiction and fantasy, in 1992, and her stories have been published everywhere from *Penthouse* to *Ms*. magazine, in *Best American Erotica*, *Best Lesbian Erotica*, and the *Mammoth Book of New Erotica*, among other places. For more juicy intimate details, she welcomes visitors to her web pages, at http://www.circlet.com/pub/u/ctan/home.html.

About the Editor: **Cara Bruce** lives in San Francisco and is the editor and founder of Venus or Vixen? and Senior Editor at GettingIt.com. Her short stories have been published in *The Unmade Bed*, *The Oy of Sex* and the forthcoming anthologies *Uniforms*, *BLE2000* and *Best Women's Erotica 2000*.